defending LOVE

ALEATHA ROMIG

NEW YORK TIMES BESTSELLING AUTHOR

Steamy, high-stakes, bodyguard, romantic-suspense stand-alone novel

ALEATHA ROMIG

New York Times, Wall Street Journal, and USA Today bestselling author

ALEATHA ROMIG'S MOST RECENT AND UPCOMING RELEASES

Visit Aleatha's store to purchase e-books, signed books, and store exclusive items.

RECENT RELEASES

DEFENDING LOVE - Standalone Novel

A steamy, high-stakes, romantic suspense with body-guard vibes, second chances, and all the feels—set in the same world as the Sinclair Duet

TO HAVE AND TO HOLD - Brutal Vows, book five - March 2025

Arranged marriage, Mafia/cartel, enemies to lovers, age-gap, he falls first, protective hero, Romeo and Juliet vibes, dangerous romance

QUEENS AND MONSTERS - Brutal Vows, book four - January 2025

Arranged marriage, Mafia/cartel, alpha hero, virgin

heroine, touch her and die, family saga, he falls first, possessive hero, sheltered heroine, dangerous romance

BOUND BY A PROMISE – Brutal Vows, book three - October 2024

Arranged marriage, age-gap, forbidden, Mafia/cartel dangerous stand-alone romance

ONE STRING – July 2024

Aleatha's Lighter Ones - Second-chance, enemies-to-lovers, fake-date, little-sister's-best-friend, forbidden, stand-alone contemporary romance

TILL DEATH DO US PART- Brutal Vows, book two - June 2024

Arranged marriage, enemies to lovers, Mafia/cartel, he falls first, stand-alone, dangerous romance

NOW AND FOREVER – Brutal Vows, book one - May 2024

Arranged marriage, age-gap, Mafia/cartel stand-alone romance

LIGHT DARK – April 2024

Cult, psychological thriller, forced proximity, romantic suspense stand-alone

*Previously published through Thomas and Mercer as INTO THE LIGHT and AWAY FROM THE DARK

REMEMBERING PASSION – Sinclair Duet book one – September 2023

Scorching hot, second-chance romance filled with the suspense and intrigue

REKINDLING DESIRE – Sinclair Duet, book two – October 2023

Scorching hot, second-chance romance filled with the suspense and intrigue

For a complete list of all Aleatha Romig's works, turn to BOOKS BY ALEATHA at the end of this novel.

DEDICATION~

This story is dedicated to the keepers of all our secrets. The only person who knows everything—our beloved hairdressers. Jane, thank you for helping me get DEFENDING LOVE going in my thoughts so it could be shared with everyone.

DEFENDING LOVE~

He's sworn to protect her. She's determined to make him stay.

I'm Elijah Rhodes, top-tier Guardian Security agent. We protect the world's power players: heads of state, royalty, A-listers. The elite.

I didn't grow up with much, and nothing came easy. My time in Special Ops hardened me, gave me purpose, and left me with a black heart. I took the missions no one else would. Still do.

My rules are simple:

No long-term assignments.

No repeats.

No attachments.

Keep it professional. Keep it distant.

It's how I've survived. Until *her*.

Dr. Danielle Sinclair is brilliant, beautiful, and off-limits. I protected her, then did what I always do. I walked away.

Now, a year later, tragedy strikes. Dani's life is in danger, and every instinct in me demands I break my own rules to keep her safe.

Some lines shouldn't be crossed.

Some rules were made to be broken.

I'll protect Dani with my life, but I can't give her a heart I don't have.

Have you been Aleatha'd?

DEFENDING LOVE is a steamy, high-stakes, bodyguard, stand-alone romantic suspense with second chances and all the feels—set in the same world as the *Sinclair Duet*.

PROLOGUE

Eli

As the elevator doors opened, I took in the entry, scanning different directions. A long receptionist's desk sat in the center with two ladies busily typing while speaking into headsets. Scrolled in large gold letters on the wall behind the women was the name Sinclair.

I searched the room for security. It appeared the only way to access the offices from this floor was through closed doors located at each end of the desk. Within the waiting area, there were clusters of chairs on carpeted surfaces and windows that showed spring's blue sky behind the Indianapolis skyline.

"May I help you?" the dark-haired receptionist

asked. After her quick scan that went from my chin-length hair to my shoes, she brightened her smile.

I wasn't unaccustomed to that assessment. Being ex-military, I worked to keep myself in top physical condition and wasn't above using my appearance for my benefit. Today wasn't such a day.

Her gaze settled momentarily on my left hand. The gold band was nothing more than a prop. Its purpose was to stop unwanted advances. It would be nice to say it worked one hundred percent of the time. It didn't. Nevertheless, I wasn't the marrying type. My career wouldn't allow it. She cleared her throat and waited for my response.

"Name is Elijah Rhodes. I have an appointment with Mr. Sinclair, Damien Sinclair."

"Yes." She jutted her chin toward the waiting area. "Please have a seat and his assistant Johnathon will be out to show you back.

"Thank you," I replied as I thought back to the call I received yesterday from Benjamin Clark, the man who brought Guardian Security Company into fruition. Since his call, I'd spent as much time as possible getting to know our potential clients. Most people who hire their own private security assumed that they were the ones deciding who to hire. The reality was that Benjamin wouldn't take on clients without approving them first. He did his homework.

There were some clients who wanted the appearance of large muscle-bound men in dark suits, wearing earpieces and surrounding them in a very public manner. While Ben had taken a few of those assignments because Guardian had men that fit that perception, he preferred clients who wanted what he sold—protection, not a show. That was why Guardian employed both men and women.

The man I was about to meet, Damien Sinclair, the CEO of Sinclair Pharmaceuticals, contacted Ben a few days ago regarding an assignment to protect his parents in Florida. Ben confided to me that as far as asshole corporate types went, Sinclair was on the cocky side, but he wasn't difficult to work with. Leo Conner, one of our best men, was point on that Florida team.

Mr. Sinclair's request increased—from what started with guarding his parents in Florida grew to also protecting his loved ones in Indianapolis, Indiana. According to Mr. Sinclair, the immediate threat was Sinclair's half-brother, Darius Sinclair, and Darius's wife, Amber.

My homework had provided background on the Sinclair family—both that which was public and that which took more skill to unravel.

Sinclair Pharmaceuticals was founded generations ago by Mr. Sinclair's great-grandfather. More recently, Mr. Sinclair's father, Derek, oversaw the company until he retired six years ago. Prior to Derek's retirement, Darius Sinclair, Derek's son from his first marriage, was named as acting CEO. It was around that time the private company began to tank.

While Sinclair Pharmaceuticals had been a

successful small company as compared to Big Pharma, it didn't see remarkable success until more recently with Damien Sinclair at the helm and the patent of Propanolol, a medication that helps people suffering from PTSD.

As a retired Special Forces weapons specialist, I knew both men and women who could benefit from such a medication if it was legitimate. Benjamin, Leo, and others on the Guardian team had similar military backgrounds.

Ben diligently watched the news of military retirements, offering jobs to those who would work best for his company. The compensation was staggering compared to that earned while in the military. Ben charged for the comfort and knowledge that those we protect were safe. In his words, that reassurance was priceless.

Taking a seat, I watched as two women exited the elevator. Ben had assigned me as point on this team, and if the job was taken, I knew who I'd be working with.

A smile threatened my serious expression at seeing the two women guards. Deidra Burton and Tara Bradley were both from the Chicago office and two of the toughest Guardians around. After speaking to the receptionist, they turned, both recognizing me immediately.

"Eli," Deidra said with a smile.

I stood as they came closer.

She lowered her voice. "My, my. Ben said he was

pulling out the big guns for this assignment." She nodded. "It's good to see you."

We shook hands.

I spoke to Tara. "I was surprised when Ben gave me your name. I thought you were working that senator's assignment in DC."

She nodded. "I am. She's currently overseas with the Secret Service. Ben said this would be a quick in-and-out assignment." Tara scoffed. "I'm not much for downtime."

Being a limited-time assignment was why I accepted Ben's offer. I didn't do long-term work. The longer a Guardian spent with a client, the more personal and the less objective our jobs became.

I'd made that mistake of getting personally involved once, and I wasn't willing to do it again.

Tara's comment about not wanting downtime was true of all of us. We weren't standing here for the money, although we'd willingly accept the checks. Performing a job like ours required dedication. That sense of devotion could only be fulfilled by the adrenaline that came from knowing your assignment was safe. Success wasn't measured in killings or gunfights.

If those occurred, it could be chalked up to an automatic loss. Wins came by avoiding or evading danger and developing a system of mutual trust.

According to Ben, Sinclair wanted both physical protection and increased technical surveillance. The threat from his brother peaked recently due to family drama. The Guardian's protection would be temporary, but the technology we left behind would keep the Sinclairs safe beyond our stay.

The three of us turned as Silas Hartman walked toward the receptionists.

"Fuck," Tara whispered. "Do you think Ben told Sinclair what this team will cost?"

"I don't think Sinclair cares," Deidra answered. "I checked out his portfolio. He has the capital. Something spooked him, and he wants to protect his wife and sister."

With a grin, Silas came toward us. "Old gang's here."

That wasn't completely true, and that memory was enough to make my smile dim.

Silas patted me on the arm. "How are you doing, Eli?"

"Fucking lethal as always."

The two women laughed.

A young man with strawberry blond hair, wearing a suit, came our direction. "Eli Rhodes?"

I took a step forward. "Yes, sir, I'm Eli Rhodes."

He offered his hand. "I'm Johnathon, Mr. Sinclair's assistant. Please follow me."

Johnathon swiped his badge to open the door to the far-right of the reception desk. The long hallway led to a set of double glass doors. Another swipe of his badge and he opened the glass doors.

Nodding, I was impressed so far by the security measures within the office.

Down the hallway, Johnathon led me through an open door. The office inside appeared to be Johnathon's space. He went to a desk and lifted a folder. Next, he knocked on one of the tall wooden-panel double doors before opening one. "Mr. Rhodes is here to see you."

While I'd expected Damien Sinclair, I wasn't expecting the two women standing near him. Mr. Sinclair came forward, his hand extended. "Mr. Rhodes, it's nice to meet you." He turned to the woman with the long dark hair wearing a skirt and blouse. "This is my wife, Ella Sinclair." I'd learned in my research that they'd only recently married. Her name was Gabriella Crystal prior to their marriage.

Next, he turned to the other woman. I sucked in a breath at her penetrating dark-blue eyes and light-brown hair. She wore a white lab coat over her blouse and slacks.

My mouth went dry.

"This is my sister, Dr. Danielle Sinclair."

Doctor.

Impressive.

I could assume that meant she was intelligent. However, I'd interacted with my share of people with an alphabet behind their names who were simultaneously inept at keeping themselves safe.

Straightening my shoulders, I nodded. "Eli, please. It's nice to meet you."

"Eli," Mr. Sinclair repeated. "Please have a seat. We'd like to ask you a few questions."

This was the part where he thought he was interviewing me.

"Leo Conner," Mr. Sinclair said, "recommended that Ella and Dani be present during this process, as if you're hired, you'll be spending your time with the two of them."

That was a good suggestion. Client compliance could make or break an assignment.

I unbuttoned my suit coat and took the chair near the windows; the other three found seats. While Damien's wife sat on the sofa at his side and to my right, Dr. Sinclair sat in a chair facing me, her gaze narrowing as if she too were assessing me.

As Mr. Sinclair began talking about how he'd found Guardian Security and that he was impressed by our standing, my gaze repeatedly went to his sister. To be completely honest, after her assessment, she appeared tired and bored.

When there was a break, I spoke to the woman across from me. "Dr. Sinclair, I excel at reading people. I'm afraid this arrangement won't work if you're not on board. I sense that this is your brother's idea, not yours."

She looked up, her eyes opening wider and her chin jutting forward. "Eli...? That's your name?"

Sassy—I was intrigued.

"Yes, Doctor, that's my name."

"My brother is a worrier. Our eldest brother is many things, but I don't believe he's dangerous."

I turned to Mr. Sinclair. "You do."

It wasn't a question. I wouldn't be here if he didn't feel his concern was warranted.

"I do." He turned to his sister. "You agreed."

She pressed her pouty lips together. "I agreed to pacify you." She waved her hand. "But now this seems unnecessary."

"Amber." Mr. Sinclair said, the name hanging in the air.

Dr. Sinclair nodded. "She's batshit crazy."

Mr. Sinclair turned to me. "Leo told me that you will be in charge of the team."

I nodded. "Correct."

"He said that the four of you have worked together on other occasions."

"We have worked together and apart. We all know one another. However, I'm not certain this assignment requires four people. It could easily be accomplished with only two for half the expense."

"Expense isn't my concern." Mr. Sinclair squeezed his wife's hand. "Safety is." He stood. "I want one person always available for Ella and one for Dani. It seems that by sharing the duties between two guards a piece, Guardian will be able to accomplish that goal."

I stood, tugging my suit coat. "Once you've had a chance to speak to everyone, we can iron out the particulars of the assignment." As my gaze found Dr. Sinclair's, she stared my direction with a mischievous grin. "Doctor, please settle this with your brother. Otherwise, we may have problems."

She sighed and looked at Mrs. Sinclair and back to

me. "The only problem will be between Damien and me. If it will stop his high blood pressure, I can agree to a short time."

A short assignment.

That was why I was here.

I bristled as I made my way back out to the waiting area. There was something about that woman—something that affected parts of me I was certain died on that fateful day. This assignment needed to be completed soon. Dr. Sinclair sparked my dried and crusty heart in a way I didn't want or need.

"Thoughts?" Silas asked as I pushed through the door and faced my team.

"I don't want to negate a possible threat." I patted him on the shoulder. "Talk to them. Give me your feedback. If we're all agreed, we can do this. We'll get the Sinclairs set up with improved technology and pacify Mr. Sinclair with a stint of hands-on driving and protection." I shrugged. "Two weeks tops." I turned to Tara. "Can you stay that long?"

"The senator will be back in a week."

"Even better," I said. "A week and we're out of Indianapolis."

CHAPTER

ONE

Marsha Sinclair
Autumn, the following year

My husband, Derek, was doing well considering that only a year ago, he'd scared us all with two heart attacks. My smile grew as I scooted into the back seat of our sedan. Derek's grin met mine as he entered from the other side.

He reached for my hand. "After lunch I'm playing nine holes with Mick."

While I enjoyed our time together after being married for nearly forty years, I was even happier to see Derek out and about, doing the things he enjoyed. "That's fine. Tonight is euchre with the Davidsons, so try to be home by five thirty."

Jack, our current bodyguard from Guardian Security turned back from the driver's seat with a nod. "To Lighthouse."

We both nodded.

Lighthouse Pointe Bar and Grille, on the shore of Lake Weir, was one of our favorite lunch spots. After Derek's health troubles, we'd been told to avoid seafood due to the high sodium. His recent improved checkup brought some of our favorite foods back onto our menu.

As tall palm trees passed by the windows, my thoughts teetered between what I'd order to eat and the snacks I would serve during tonight's card game. It was our turn to host, and I was certain our guests would be happy that Derek's improved health would allow for more indulgent delicacies.

"Traffic is heavier than expected," Jack announced.

A peek out the window shield revealed a trail of illuminated taillights.

"I wonder what the holdup could be," Derek said. "What?" My husband's attention turned to the side window.

I didn't see the man until Derek hit the button to lower the pane.

What I noticed first was a cardboard sign held by an elderly man. "You're Derek Sinclair?"

My flesh prickled with a sudden chill. "Who's asking?"

He leaned closer, dark eyes piercing and his dirty

graying hair disheveled, as he confirmed, "Sinclair Pharmaceuticals?"

The encounter lasted only seconds. Jack turned from the front seat to see what was happening.

"I am," Derek replied.

The cardboard sign lowered. A reflection of sunlight shimmered on the barrel of the gun. It was the realization that occurred milliseconds before the popping sound. Derek flew backward toward me. Pain came seconds after the sight of blood on my blouse. The last thing I remembered was Jack opening his car door.

My world went black.

CHAPTER

TWO

Dani

Two weeks later

S hivering, I walked along the uneven ground and took my seat, the one beside my brother Damien. The blue sky above us was deceiving, an autumn sapphire hue promising warmth. Instead, as the Indiana breeze blew the colorful leaves like a cyclone, heat failed to materialize. My circulation chilled.

Damien reached over and covered my hand with his. I didn't look up. I couldn't. My bloodshot eyes were fixed permanently on the ornate wooden coffin only a few feet in front of us. After two weeks, the Sumter County Coroner's Office in Florida finally released our father's body.

The empty chair to my other side was supposed to be occupied by our mother, Marsha Sinclair. Thankfully, she was alive. Unfortunately, she was still lying in a hospital bed behind a guarded door. The men behind us in black suits were present for the same reason, protecting those of us who remained of Derek Sinclair's legacy—Sinclair Pharmaceuticals. Their presence did little to reassure me. Instead, it grated on me, like fingernails over a chalkboard.

Dad had security; he had since his health scare a year ago. Damien insisted upon it. Little good it did. From what Jack, the bodyguard, told us, the assailant appeared next to Dad's car as our parents were on their way out to lunch in the Villages, a wealthy Florida suburb.

What we've been able to learn from the police and traffic cameras was that a man who appeared elderly with a sign asking for donations was on the median on a well-traveled roadway. Dad rolled down his window. The man confirmed our father's name and then without warning, fired two shots. One killed our father instantly, the second hit Mom, becoming wedged near her spinal cord.

The guard in the driver's seat was caught unprepared. By the time he had his pistol out, the assailant disappeared, running back through stopped traffic and vanishing.

It didn't make sense.

Two weeks and the case was going cold.

Retired CEO of Sinclair Pharmaceuticals shot dead in broad daylight.

The best the police could tell us was that they didn't believe it was a random act of violence. Dad was targeted.

We didn't know by whom or why.

Our only clue was that the assailant confirmed Dad's identity and his association with Sinclair Pharmaceuticals seconds before firing his gun.

Our mother would recover. Currently, she was still in a Florida hospital, soon being moved to rehab. The damage to her spinal cord resulted in the need for physical therapy. Damien, his wife, Ella, Dad's friend and attorney, Stephen Elliott, and I flew down immediately. The doctors said it was too early to send her from Florida back to Indiana for Dad's funeral.

Ella, my sister-in-law, sat on Damien's other side, holding their two-month-old son, Dylan Sinclair, whose cries reflected my mood. As the minister stepped up to the coffin, Ella's mother came forward, taking Dylan from Ella's arms and shushing his whimpers.

Mom asked us to keep Dad's ceremony small. Minus the bodyguards, only a few close friends, and members of the Sinclair executive board who had known Dad for years were in attendance; we kept our promise.

As the minister was about to speak, Darius, our father's son from his first marriage, made his way to our mother's empty chair.

"Get the fuck away from here," Damien growled.

Damien and Darius's feud had intensified since our father's murder. Meaning it went from one hundred to two hundred and ten in the course of a conversation. Damien suspected Darius's involvement in our father's death.

"He was my father too," Darius quipped.

I lifted both of my hands, trying to momentarily deflect the ensuing daggers. "I'm not sitting in the middle of this." I met Damien's dangerously dark gaze. "Not now."

The muscles in the side of Damien's face pulled taut. I peered around him, silently pleading to Ella. She reached for my brother's arm and laced hers through his bent elbow. It wasn't an end to the feud between the two men on either side of me, but by the way Damien exhaled, it seemed a small reprieve.

A gentleman in a dark suit appeared. "Mr. Sinclair." He spoke to Darius. "As we told you at the funeral home, your presence is a violation of Mr. Sinclair's restraining order."

I turned to Damien, my lips pressed together.

A restraining order?

My brother's words didn't match the guttural growl to his voice. "He can stay until the ceremony is complete."

The bodyguard nodded. "I'll be happy to escort you once the ceremony is done." He then stepped to Darius's side.

"Very generous of you, brother," Darius mumbled.

He leaned closer to me. "Dani, you know I'm heart-broken too."

Shaking my head, I looked down at my hands folded in my lap. While their trembling had ceased, the bone-chilling cold remained.

"Family and friends," the minister began. "As we remember Derek..."

If I were quizzed on what was said earlier during the funeral or currently at the gravesite, I would fail miserably. My thoughts were filled with memories of the man who was a husband and a dad. Despite running a successful pharmaceutical company, he never shied away from fatherly duties. I couldn't recall a time he or Mom missed one of my swimming meets or one of Damien's basketball games.

He encouraged my love of science. That passion led me to study chemistry and biology. The double major, master's degree, and ensuing PhD secured my role in our family company. Vice president in charge of research and development was my current title.

My thoughts had gone to happier times—years of vacationing on Florida's west coast, probably the reason our parents later chose to move to the Sunshine State—when the minister handed me a long-stemmed rose. It took me a moment to rationalize where I was and why he handed it to me. Peering around, I saw that Ella was also holding one as she stood. I rose to meet her next to the coffin. A lump formed in my throat as we both laid the flowers on top of the shiny, smooth wood.

I blinked away the tears.

It was as I turned back toward my seat that my breath caught. Standing with the other guards was a man who hadn't been there earlier, not once during the last two horrible weeks.

Eli Rhodes stood inches above the other guards, his shoulders wide. The cut of his expensive dark suit accentuated his toned chest and V-shaped torso. Emotions cycloned within me as my mouth went suddenly dry.

With his hands clasped before him and working to maintain his elusive stare, Eli's veneer cracked just a little as his green gaze met mine.

Memories of our short time together cascaded through my mind as I unsuccessfully fought off the tears. Fresh, salty streams sizzled on my cold cheeks as I gasped for breath.

Ella reached for my elbow, pulling me back to present. "Sit down, Dani," she whispered.

Nodding, I took my seat, aware of the presence of the last man I'd had feelings for and the warmth of his stare on the back of my head.

CHAPTER

THREE

Dani

As Darius stood, the man in the dark suit approached. Darius lifted his hands and turned toward the rest of us who were also standing. "I didn't have anything to do with what happened to Dad and Marsha."

Damien's jaw clenched. "The police and our security are investigating every possible lead."

Darius turned to me. "Dani, talk some sense into him. He's wasting time when the real threat is still out there." He scoffed. "He could be right there." Darius jutted his chin toward Damien.

"Stop with the accusations." I took a step back. "Stay safe, Darius. If this person's motive has anything to do with Sinclair Pharmaceuticals, you could be on their radar."

He smirked and jutted his chin toward Damien. "He's done all he can do to alienate me from Sinclair. Now, with Dad gone, I'm sure he'll do what he can to take over my stock. Maybe I should take his offer. Getting away from this company could save my life." He reached for my arm and lowered his voice. "Damien's an asshole but listen to him about security. You could also be on the assailant's radar."

"Escort our brother off the premises," Damien said. He gazed around as mourners made their way to their cars. "Where's Dylan?"

"Mom took him to the car to stay warm," Ella replied. She reached for my hand. "Are you all right? Earlier, you looked pale."

"Tired," I said with a sigh. "I want to go to bed for the next month, but I really should head down to Florida and check on Mom."

"We need to call a board meeting," Damien said. "We should let the members know the status of business affairs regarding Dad's passing."

The three of us walked away from the casket as workers prepared to lower it into the vault. Due to Indiana's rainfall, all caskets were sealed in concrete vaults to avoid them springing to the surface during highwater.

"Grace Haas is out of the country," I replied. "Without Dad and Mom, there won't be a quorum."

"If Mom gives you proxy, we can address filling Dad's spot."

Closing my eyes, I exhaled. "Can it wait until next Monday? Surely, no one expects us to meet following the funeral."

"It's been two weeks," Ella reminded us. "We don't have any problem members of the board, not since Gloria Wilmott resigned."

That was a story for another day, a day when I had more energy. In a nutshell, Gloria attempted to blackmail Damien into marrying her daughter Amber. Thankfully, the two Wilmotts had slipped away, hopefully, under some rock.

Our conversation ended as Art Hatfield and Rachel Stokes came closer. Art was the treasurer of the Sinclair Pharmaceuticals executive board and Rachel was the secretary. "Our condolences," Rachel said with sympathy in her gaze. "Derek was..." She inhaled. "He'll be missed."

"Thank you," I replied. "Rachel, do you think it would be out of line to wait to convene the executive board until next week. I want to get down to Mom for a few days."

Rachel reached for my hand. "Marsha should come first. I'll call the other members of the board." She turned to Damien. "I'm assuming as CEO, you agree with this schedule."

Damien nodded as Stephen Elliott, a friend of Dad's and the head of Sinclair legal, joined us.

"I can't believe he's gone," Stephen said.

It was a sentiment we'd heard over and over.

Stephen lowered his voice. "I know now isn't the time, but I wanted to remind you that Preston Ayers would be a perfect addition to the executive board."

I shook my head, unwilling to give mind space to Dad's replacement.

Damien stood taller. "As in the Preston Ayers who was the dean of research at Indianapolis University?"

"Preston's running for governor and could be a powerful ally for tax incentives. He's looking to make his name better known."

"Stephen, this isn't the time," I said. "Send us his CV, and we can look it over." With that, the three of us turned toward the waiting car.

Ella's mother stepped from the funeral home's limousine as we neared. She gave Ella and me a hug. "You all need some rest."

By the pounding in my temples, I knew she was right.

Mrs. Crystal turned to Ella. "Dylan's all buckled in."

"Thanks, Mom."

Making my way into the limousine, I took in the interior and briefly wondered how many grieving families had ridden in this same vehicle. The woman entering the seat next to the driver looked familiar.

As I stared her way, Ella settled next to Dylan's car seat and followed my line of sight. "Deidra Burton from Guardian Security. She worked with me for a short time last year."

"She's back? I thought Guardian didn't do repeat assignments."

"I spoke with Benjamin Clark right after Dad's murder," Damien said as the car began to move, driving slowly through the large cemetery. "I asked if any of our previous bodyguards were available. At first, everyone was assigned elsewhere. Benjamin did whatever he does. Ms. Burton and Mr. Rhodes were reassigned to us."

My lips pressed together.

Damien cocked his head to the side. "I thought you'd be happy. Eli is someone you know. He can accompany you to Florida."

I lowered my voice. "I wish you would have spoken to me first. I'm fine with one of the other ones. Melinda has been with me for the last two weeks."

"She has another assignment that needed her to return."

That was what Eli said when he left a year ago—that he had another assignment. It wasn't the only reason he left. Truly, at that time, Damien's paranoia and overprotectiveness was unjustified. Darius and Amber pulled some stupid shit like breaking into our respective homes and planting cameras, but they weren't a true danger.

Now things were different.

As the air around us rippled with tension, we were all well aware that this time, the danger was real.

My gaze went to Dylan, his eyes closed as the pacifier in his mouth moved in and out. "Ella and Dylan need the protection. Eli can work for them."

Ella grinned at her husband. "Your insecure brother prefers I don't have hot bodyguards."

"I'm not insecure," Damien said with a grin.

"Truth is that I asked for Deidra," Ella said. "She's effective and low stress. I don't need any uncomfortableness added to my plate, especially with nursing Dylan." She leaned forward. "I know we joke about how good-looking Eli is, but I thought you felt the same."

That he's handsome...yes.

That in the short time he was assigned to me, he wore down some of my insecurities about having him around. And also, that when he abruptly left with no further contact, I was affected more than I wanted to admit.

I sat taller. "It's just a job, right?"

"Right," Damien said. "Once the perp is found, we can go back to normal."

With the lack of progress the police have made, his statement sounded like an impossible timeline.

"Have you thought," I asked, "if Dad's case could be like the insurance CEO in New York? Do you think someone is upset about one of our drugs?"

"Saline and insulin have been around for decades," Damien said.

I had a thought. "Could it be Propanolol? If the

person suffered from PTSD…" I left the sentence open-ended.

Propanolol not only saved Sinclair Pharmaceuticals after Darius almost ran the company into the ground, but it propelled our small company from obscure to a bona fide player in the pharmaceutical world.

Damien nodded. "I've spoken with the detectives in Florida and members of the FBI. Ella is working with Johnathon to find physicians prescribing Propanolol and work from there. There is a national database." He exhaled. "However, that's only a drop in the bucket. Propanolol is prescribed throughout the world."

Ella spoke up as her gaze met mine. "I don't want to think that one of the Sinclair formulas was the motive." She shook her head. "Until we know for sure, we all need to be extra-vigilant."

"Have there been any lawsuits, filings against Sinclair?" I asked.

Ella shrugged. "There's always something. But that's a good idea. Johnathon and I will look at that angle and see if we can find a lead."

The limousine pulled up in front of the building in downtown Indy that housed my condominium. As the driver opened the door, I noticed the black sedan pulling up behind the long vehicle. Stepping out of the sedan was none other than my new—old—body-guard, Elijah Rhodes.

Securing my sunglasses over my eyes, I squared

my shoulders and took a deep breath as my shoes hit the pavement.

I could do this.

It was just his job.

Nothing more.

Eli

D r. Danielle Sinclair was even more beautiful than I remembered. When her tear-filled, navy-blue stare met mine at the gravesite, it took all my self-control to remain professional. My body yearned to step forward, wrap her in my arms, shield her from the pain of losing her father, and warm her from the cool autumn temperatures. There was more in her eyes than sadness. This attack on her father was an attack on her family and their family business.

It was an attack on all the Sinclairs.

When Ben called, I was finishing up an assignment out of the country. As a rule, I shied away from guarding celebrities. The publicity, the frenzied fans, and the entitled attitudes weren't qualities I found conducive to the job. My last assignment wasn't supposed to be like that. She was a bestselling author on a book tour. Her book had only recently been released, but almost instantaneously, it blew up. Mobs of readers lined sidewalks around bookstores for hours. Unsuspecting stores turned into something akin to a rock concert.

In my opinion, the tour couldn't end soon enough.

The only positive about the assignment was that the author herself wasn't an entitled diva. On the contrary, she was an introvert. Convincing her to stay in her hotel room with only her PR staff wasn't difficult. She preferred the solitude to sightseeing or making unplanned appearances.

Dr. Sinclair stepped from the limousine, her shapely legs coming into view. My gaze moved upward as the black skirt of her dress fluttered in the breeze. Golden streaks shimmered in her light brown hair that was now pulled back into a low ponytail. While I was haunted by her stunning blue eyes at the cemetery, currently they were obscured by her sunglasses.

"I'll call you once Dr. Sinclair is settled," I said to Larry Floyd, the point on this assignment.

Larry nodded. "I was surprised you said yes to Ben's request."

His comment caused my skin to tighten. Taking on the same assignment for a second time wasn't my usual.

Larry continued, "I've never known you to repeat an assignment."

"I guess I surprised everyone." Even me.

Larry was correct. When it came to assignments, I was known for not forming attachments. Connections muddied the already-murky water. I'd made that mistake at the other end of this business. My hardened heart forbade me from repeating it.

However, the sight of Danielle crying near her father's grave solidified my resolve that returning to Dr. Sinclair was the right decision. The confident, sexual woman I'd met over a year ago—the chemist, the researcher, the eloquently spoken businesswoman with knowledge beyond my comprehension, and the woman that heated my blood—was buried beneath her grief and fear.

The fire within her wasn't gone. It couldn't be. That heat was too fierce to disappear. It was simply dimmed. This emotional state was not where I would or could leave her.

I stepped forward, meeting Dr. Sinclair on the sidewalk.

"Eli."

My hand twitched, wanting to reach out to her. Instead, I remained stoic. "Dr. Sinclair."

She looked around the sidewalk, as if hesitating to say what was on her mind. Finally, with a shrug, she said, "I guess you know the way."

With a nod, I walked at her side through the glass doors. With each step toward the elevator, I scanned the large first-level entrance. There was a coffee shop on the right with customers paying no attention to those walking by. The glass door of the boutique on the left was closed. Up ahead was a restaurant bustling with lunch patrons. We turned into the hallway with the bank of elevators.

After pushing the button, Dr. Sinclair stood back, staring at the door in front of her as the numbers on the display lowered. The riders disembarked, leaving the elevator car empty.

It wasn't until we stepped inside and the doors closed that I spoke. "I talked to Melinda."

The elevator began to rise, and Danielle nodded. "I didn't know she was being replaced."

There was a distinct chill to her tone.

"I would have come sooner, but I was on assignment."

"It's your job, Eli. I get that." She turned toward me, her damn eyes still covered with the dark sunglasses. "Why come back here? To me?"

Because I couldn't stay away.

That wasn't my answer. I shook my head. "Because ever since I heard about your father, I've been concerned. This isn't like last time, Doctor. Last time your brother was overreacting or maybe it was a power move to show the other Mr. Sinclair what he could do to keep his loved ones safe."

She didn't respond. Instead, Danielle sniffled and ran the top of her hand below her nose. The doors opened to the familiar hallway.

I kept in step with her. "There is a real possibility of present danger."

With a stiff chin, she nodded as she continued walking toward the door to her condominium. As she reached for the keypad, I stopped her.

"I've changed your code."

Danielle took a step back, inhaled sharply, and stared incredulously at me. "Without consulting me?"

"Melinda and I discussed it." I entered the code. "The fewer people who know, the better."

"Maybe I could be included on that list?"

"You will be." After entering the new code, I tipped my chin and looked up and down the empty hallway. "Stay here a moment, Doctor. I'll do a sweep."

"My name is Dani. I think we've passed the formality."

A punch to the gut.

We had passed that formality. That was my mistake.

When I didn't respond, she pressed her lips together and tilted her head toward the open door. "How could anyone be inside there? You're the only one who knows the code."

Leave no stone unturned.

"Please wait a moment." Removing my gun from my side holster, I entered the condominium. The security upgrade we did last year had been cutting edge, but technology has improved quickly. I would make a few adjustments to bring it up to speed.

The large floor-to-ceiling windows filled the front

room and kitchen with sunlight. A smile threatened to curl my lips at the sight of the gray walls, white trim, and stylish furniture. Everything about this home reflected Dani Sinclair's style and need for control.

The immaculate kitchen glistened from the stainless-steel appliances to the granite countertops. Down the first hallway, I checked the bathroom, laundry room, second bedroom, and office.

The small office was the only room that wasn't spotless. Her desk had stacks of notes and there was a coffee cup to the side of the monitors. Back through the living room, I entered the primary bedroom. Her bed was meticulously made, even the throw pillows were in place. Inside her attached bathroom, every towel was hanging as if it were a hotel on check-in day.

"Come in," I called as I again neared the door to the hallway.

With an exaggerated huff, she entered.

I closed the door and set the lock.

Dani laid her purse on the counter, kicked off her high-heeled shoes, and picked them up. "I'm exhausted. I'm going to take a shower and lie down for a little while. I have work to do here. If I'm really your assignment, tomorrow we're headed to the Villages. I know the routine. You can book our flight and two hotel rooms."

"Why won't you take the company plane?"

"Because it's extravagant to take the plane when it's only two people."

"Traveling commercial?" I said with a questioning tone. "If the suspect is halfway decent at hacking, he's probably watching for your or Mr. Sinclair's name to pop up on a manifest headed for Florida, knowing you'll be checking in on your mother."

"Then he'd also have someone watching private airports for the Sinclair plane."

"Statistically, there's a better chance of him being a lone wolf. Those are also historically more difficult to find."

Dani removed her sunglasses and laid them next to her purse. When she turned my direction, I saw the redness and puffiness in and around her eyes.

"I know I look like shit. My head is throbbing."

She was wrong. Danielle Sinclair was still staggeringly beautiful even with her defenses down. "Follow through with your plan." I lifted my palm toward her. "I need to assess your phone and access the computer in your home office."

"Melinda already did that."

"Dani," I said, forgoing the formality, "you are my assignment, now *my* responsibility. I trust Melinda as much as I do any of the members of Guardian Security, but when it's my job, I do it my way."

She went to her purse and pulled out her phone. "Fine," she said, handing it to me. "Do you need the passcode, or have you changed that too?"

"I haven't yet."

She shook her head as she turned toward her bedroom. There was an unusual slump to her shoulders and posture. For a few brief seconds when she first spoke on the sidewalk and again when she learned I'd changed her security code, the sassy, strong woman was back.

"Dani?"

She turned around and faced me.

For a split second, I focused on her lips, remembering the hunger in her kiss. I blinked and saw her gaze. That kiss was why I left her before. I shouldn't even think about it. "You're going to be safe. Your brother and his family will be safe and your mother too. The police are working on your father's case, but so are we. Guardian Security is one of the best. You will get your life back."

"But not my father." She turned and closed the bedroom door behind her.

Not her father.

Another punch to the gut.

Dani was right. I couldn't get her father back, but I could keep her safe.

CHAPTER
FIVE

Dani

After closing the bedroom door, I dropped my shoes and flopped back on the bed with my eyes closed. Eli's words ran through my thoughts—get my life back.

What was my life?

Work.

I loved my work in the Sinclair labs or sitting behind a computer. Research opened a door in my soul that longed to be filled. I craved more information, new discoveries, and revealing what was previously unknown. Dad encouraged that part of me, saying that he wished he shared my unbridled thirst for knowledge.

Dad.

The question I asked Damien and Ella came back to me. Could Dad's murder be a disgruntled patient or family member of a patient related to our marketed products? My thoughts went to Propanolol.

I officially became a significant part of Sinclair Pharmaceuticals after completing my PhD in pharmacological research. Before that time, I spent any time I could with the Sinclair chemists who created the revolutionary compound. Dr. David Carpenter was our primary researcher. The work with Propanolol was more exciting than anything being done at the university.

In the Sinclair labs, Dr. Carpenter and the other scientists isolated the organic compound propanolamine and mutated it at positions one and three. Prior to coming to Sinclair, Dr. Carpenter had connections to another scientist who had been working on a similar project at a small university. That research was shut down, a funding issue I was told.

Truly, without David's previous knowledge, Sinclair's Propanolol wouldn't exist. Currently, it was the top compound for treating post-traumatic stress disorder. As a treatment for PTSD, many assumed that Propanolol erased memories; it didn't.

Instead, the compound interrupted the sequence of memories, causing a favorable pairing as opposed to a negative one. What made it remarkable was that not everyone had the same trigger and yet we found success.

During earlier trials, there were military veterans

who had different triggers. There was one man who couldn't watch fireworks. During battle, fireworks were used for communication before an offensive. The different colors told the soldiers what was going to happen. There was another volunteer who suffered serious injuries in a car accident. Simply getting into a car was torture. The formula worked in both cases.

If a consumer didn't receive the anticipated relief from Propanolol, that should have been observed by the physician and psychiatrist. They would then be able to adjust dosages. Monitoring of patients was crucial in prescribing Propanolol.

How or why would a person hunt down the retired CEO?

It didn't make sense.

Not that I wanted my brother to be harmed, but Damien was the current CEO and the man responsible for bringing Dr. David Carpenter to Sinclair.

Could the assailant be someone who worked for Dad?

The more I thought, the more questions came to mind.

It was a never-ending cycle.

Forcing myself from the comfortable bed, I stripped out of my black dress and sheer tights before making my way into the bathroom. Dropping my bra and panties on the bathroom floor, I turned the shower's dial to hot. Under the prickling spray, I lifted my chin, letting the water pelt my face as tears returned.

My life back.

My work.

My family.

My security.

By the time I turned off the shower, my fingertips were pruney, but for the moment, I was out of tears. Wiping the steam from the mirror over the vanity, I stared into my own bloodshot eyes. A few eyedrops and the redness lessened.

After covering my face with moisturizer, I combed my wet long hair. It was as I slipped into a soft pair of shorts and an oversized shirt that I remembered my bodyguard. It wasn't like I could forget him; I simply needed to say my own goodbye to Dad before I could face the present.

Life needed me to move forward. It was what my father would have wanted.

Another glance in the mirror told me that I should dress more appropriately. My shorts were short, and I wasn't wearing a bra. I inhaled, noticing the way the shirt tented over my nipples.

To hell with that.

Ella had gotten the bodyguard that made her life less complicated. I got the man that was nothing but complicated.

If Eli Rhodes agreed to infiltrate my life, he'd need to deal with me as I was. And at this moment, this was who I was.

Opening the door to my bedroom, I spotted Eli sitting at the breakfast counter, the one separating the kitchen from the living room. His attention was focused on his tablet, leaving him unaware that I'd reentered the living room.

There was a theory about mind and body memories that surfaced in our research. While both forms of memories were largely based on reality, the human brain had the unique ability to amplify or diminish said memories, much the same as researchers who created gene sequencing to revive previously extinct creatures. When missing all the original DNA, substitute DNA, like that from a frog, could be used to fill in the blanks.

Our memories were similar. We received a stimulus—a sight or a scent—and it had the power to bring back memories, creating projections within our thoughts. If we didn't recall every detail, our mind filled in the blanks.

Over the last year, I wondered if I'd elaborated my memories of Elijah Rhodes.

Had I made him into more of a man than he was?

As I stood silently and stared at his brown hair tied into a short ponytail at the nape of his neck, his wide shoulders, and then lower to his trim waist where his white shirt was tucked into his black pants, I realized the truth. I hadn't exaggerated my recollections. If anything, I'd minimized them. Perhaps it was a survival technique.

To have meticulously recalled a man I never expected to see again—a man like Eli—would be to forever compare every other man to him. To date, I'd yet to meet anyone who came remotely close.

I'd successfully suppressed the memory of our kiss and the fire in his touch—until now.

My breathing deepened, pressing my breasts against the material of my shirt. Darting my tongue to my lips, I recalled the ferocity of his pressing down on mine.

My memories, completely restored and without elaboration, were back with a vengeance, warming my circulation and twisting my core.

Eli turned, his shimmering green eyes scanning from my bare feet up to my wet hair, and a grin tugged at his lips. "Do you feel better?"

Inhaling, I nodded. "I didn't nap, but the shower was good."

He stepped from the stool.

It was my turn to scan. Starting with shiny dark shoes, long legs clad in black pants, up to a black belt, I pressed my lips together. His white button-up shirt was unbuttoned at the neck, and his tie and jacket from earlier were missing. The ring on his left hand caught my attention. He'd worn it before, but then it wasn't anything other than decoration to deter advances so as to keep his attention on the job.

Eli must have followed my gaze. He lifted his hand and spun the gold band. "I didn't marry if that's what you're wondering."

"None of my business."

"Neither have you."

"None of your business."

"Technically, as your bodyguard, it would be my business."

I took a few steps closer. "I thought when you left last time, you said you didn't believe in long-term or repeat assignments."

His head moved from side to side. "Fuck, Dani. Don't read more into this than it is. Your father was murdered, and I wanted to be sure you were safe."

One more step closer and the woodsy scent of his cologne tickled my senses. "I wasn't safe with Melinda?"

"She couldn't stay."

"You don't trust your fellow bodyguards at Guardian Security?"

Eli came closer still, causing me to lift my chin to maintain eye contact. It was when his palm gently cupped my cheek that I closed my eyes, feeling his touch tingle throughout my already-warmed circulation. When I opened my eyes, he was close enough for me to feel the radiating heat from his hard body. "I never should have kissed you." His nostrils flared. "Before. It was wrong."

I swallowed the disappointment I knew was in store and took a step back. "Don't worry. I'm only a job. You made that clear."

"Did you tell anyone about the kiss?"

I shook my head.

His green eyes hooded as he peered down at the floor and back up to meet my gaze. "I'm not like that, Dani. I've worked for Ben for almost ten years, and I've never gotten personal with a client."

"Never?"

"Not a client." His nostrils flared. "Just you, and I did what I could to correct it."

"You left," I said matter-of-factly.

Eli nodded. "I was a fucking coward."

My lips quirked. "Then you're definitely in the wrong profession."

"I can take on any danger. I've faced death more times than I can remember. I don't get frightened easily, but there's something about you. You scare the shit out of me."

"Then why come ba—"

He interrupted, his tone deepening. "Because the idea of anyone harming you is incomprehensible."

"Eli, I'm going to be completely honest with you. Right now, I'm too fragile to allow my heart the opportunity to break."

"I can see that."

Exhaling, I took another step away and slapped my hands against my thighs. "I told you; I look like shit."

"You look fucking scrumptious, even when you're fragile. You're fiercely radiant when you're strong." He inhaled. "For this to work" —he motioned between us — "for me to keep you safe, I need to know you still trust me and you understand that while I'm breaking my own rule by taking this job, I'll only stay as long as you need my protection."

"A job," I repeated.

"A job I won't fail. Ben has rules. They're there for good reasons. I can't break them again. I know you're off-limits. Our relationship will be professional. Can you trust me again?"

There was a lot to unpack in his statement.

"I thought you said you were never personal with another client. What rule did you break?"

His jaw clenched, and his Adam's apple bobbed. "It wasn't a client. Can you trust me?"

Could I trust him?

"To keep me safe?" I nodded. "I can do that. I think you're hiding something, something you don't want to share. That's fine. I'm only a job. I won't trust you with my heart."

The spark in his eyes dimmed. "That's best. Now, let me tell you our travel plans."

CHAPTER
SIX

Dani

"I'll be back Sunday night," I said to my brother Damien through the phone.

"Eli is traveling with you?"

"Yes, I'm not fighting the bodyguard thing."

Damien exhaled. "FaceTime me when you're with Mom. Tell her we love her and want her to get better. Hey, tell her to consider moving back to Indy."

"Are you sure you and Ella want Mom in your newlywed home?"

"With Dylan, there's not a lot of newlywed activity." He snickered. "Maybe Mom could babysit, and I could get some."

"Way too much info, brother." There was a knock

on my bedroom door. "I need to go. I'll keep you updated with text messages."

"Dani, one more thing. Take the plane. It's available."

"Eli already booked our flights." I forced a smile. "Give Dylan a kiss from Aunt Dani. And no, I won't babysit so you can screw your wife. Work that shit out on your own."

"Stay safe," he said as another knock rattled the door.

"You too." I disconnected the call and spoke louder. "You can come in, Eli." It wasn't rocket science to guess who was knocking—the only other person in the condominium.

The sight of Eli in bodyguard mode took my breath away. Wearing one of his custom dark suits, Eli's brown hair was tethered at the nape of his neck, showcasing his high cheekbones and chiseled jaw.

After doing a sweep from my shoes to my hair, his green gaze was set on mine. "Larry is a few minutes away. He's driving us to the airport."

I closed the zipper on my suitcase. "I'm ready."

His eyebrows arched. "Only one suitcase?"

"I have my laptop and other electronics in the leather satchel."

His brow furrowed. "Laptop?"

"Yes. Is there a problem?"

"You didn't mention it yesterday. I didn't look through your laptop, only your desktop and phone."

Placing the suitcase on the floor, I secured the

satchel over the extended handle. "I told you Melinda went through them all."

"You should have mentioned it."

Squaring my shoulders, I pointed to the leather bag. "Feel free to inspect it at the airport after we go through security."

I spun my suitcase and moved toward the doorway.

"Dani, I can get your luggage."

"So can I. I'm not sure if you remember, but I'm not one of your spoiled, entitled assignments. I'm capable of doing most things on my own."

My nipples hardened as I recalled touching myself last night, thinking about the man now only inches away.

Capable was not always the better alternative.

Eli's timbre lowered an octave. "I remember many things about you."

Ignoring the way his lowered tone reverberated through my body, sending mini explosions throughout my nervous system, I pushed the suitcase past him out into the living room. My gaze went to the large windowpanes, taking in the gray clouds and drizzling rain. "At least it should be sunny in Florida."

"The flights are booked primarily under my name with a Guardian credit card," Eli said. "The same with the villa at the resort. It's more private than hotel rooms and safer with private parking."

I wasn't about to fight him on any of those fronts. Damien hadn't told me how much he paid for the services of the Guardian Security Company, but I was confident that Guardian wouldn't come out on the short end of the deal.

Despite my willingness to steer my own luggage, Eli took both my bag and his own and wheeled them to the door.

Ten minutes later, I was seated in the back seat of a large black SUV, and Eli was sitting shotgun. Speaking of guns, flying commercially made it more difficult for Eli to carry his weapon. Last night, after we'd ordered delivery and were eating chicken cordon bleu from a small place on East New York Street, he mentioned the dilemma.

It wasn't like I couldn't have cooked. I had when he was assigned to me last year. It was that through the trauma of the last two weeks, grocery shopping was low on my list of priorities, and my cupboards were bare.

The dilemma, Eli explained, was that in the case of flying commercially, TSA made transporting a weapon difficult. The solution—a member of the Guardian team would pick us up from the airport and assign Eli working weapons for our time in Florida. I knew from my limited experience that his arsenal would be more than simply a gun. Besides the firearms, the team would have Eli's hotel room set up as a home-away-from-home computer base.

Was it wrong that merely having him with me, even without a gun, settled my nerves?

My phone vibrated. I opened the screen to a text

message from my mother. I spent over an hour talking to her last night trying to settle her angst at missing Dad's funeral.

"I was just informed they're moving me at 2 pm today to the physical-rehab facility in the Villages. What time did you say you expect to arrive?"

I couldn't blame her for not remembering. She had more than enough on her own plate. I replied.

"Plane lands in Orlando at 2:45 pm. Text me the address of the new facility."

She sent a thumbs-up emoji.

Beyond the windows of the SUV, the dreary day accurately reflected my gray mood. Focusing on the man in the front seat didn't do my emotions any better. Each time I recalled him telling me not to read more into his assignment than there was, I was reminded that Eli Rhodes was only here because I was a job. Even if he was concerned, that wouldn't be reflected in anything other than his duties.

Larry brought the SUV to a stop in front of the 'departures' sign at Indianapolis International Airport. After retrieving our luggage, Eli and I entered the airport. As he scanned the crowd, he whispered, "Stay close."

My pulse thumped within my ears as I realized that I too now saw people differently than I had in the past. Never before had I minded taking commercial flights, walking a few blocks to a restaurant, or entering a sports arena filled with thousands of people.

In the last two weeks all that had changed. Every person was a suspect. I imagined people looking in my direction, hundreds of eyes on me. Even small children turned their faces toward me and away.

Had they seen me on the news or in their media feed?

Did they know I was the daughter of the slain CEO?

I held my breath waiting for a reaction as I passed my driver's license to the woman at the airline counter. She glanced at the picture and back to me before handing it back. I exhaled. The TSA pre-check line moved painfully slowly. The same anxiety hit me as I once again handed over my ID. This time the man scanned it.

No obvious indication of recognition.

It wasn't until we were walking down the hallway toward the gates that Eli asked, "Are you all right?"

The question was laughable.

There was nothing about me that was all right.

I'd just buried my father and was on my way to my mourning and injured mother.

Instead, I responded, "I'm fine."

He nodded. "If I'd just met you, I could believe that."

I stopped walking and turned to him, lifting my chin to meet his stare. "I'm a little slow with all that's happened. Are we or aren't we pretending the past never occurred? Because your statement makes it seem like we have a history."

"A history where I can't recall you being as tense as you've been since we entered the airport."

Pressing my lips together, I shook my head. It was all too much. My skin felt tight. Another couple walked around us, the woman's shoulder brushing mine, causing me to flinch. "I'm not talking about this right now."

"Then by all means, let's go to the gate. Boarding begins in less than a half hour."

As we sat at the gate in the connected black chairs, I varied between searching every face and keeping my eyes down.

Eli's deep voice returned me to reality. "I'd like to see your laptop."

Begrudgingly and with a sigh, I took it from my satchel and handed it to him.

Without asking, he turned it on, entering my security code.

"How do you know that?" I asked.

"I helped you set it up."

"And you remember it?"

He nodded as he pulled a thumb drive from his satchel and inserted it into the side of my computer.

Within seconds, the screen was filled with scrolling letters and numbers.

"I have files I don't want to lose."

"It's searching, not deleting."

The sign behind the woman at the desk said boarding would begin in thirteen minutes. I wondered how long whatever Eli was doing would take. Peering down at the screen, I nibbled on my lip as the data continued to scroll.

I wasn't certain what was slower, watching the fast-moving file names and numbers or waiting for the boarding time to decrease.

Finally, the data disappeared, and a small rectangle appeared. "What did you learn?"

Eli didn't answer. Instead, he typed on the keyboard.

The sign now read nine minutes. People were beginning to stand. The woman behind the desk made another announcement about carry-on bags, offering to check them for free.

Eli slid my laptop back into my satchel and sent off a text message.

The pressure within me was beginning to reach a boiling point.

"What did you find?" I whispered with a growl of discontent.

"The same thing I found on your phone and desktop."

"Nothing?"

"We can talk about it when we're in private."

"Are you trying to freak me out?"

He lowered his voice. "I'm trying *not* to freak you out."

"Well, you're not doing a good job."

"Dani, look at me."

Exhaling, I did. I turned and stared into the tranquil green of his eyes.

"You're safe," he said. "Once we're back to Indianapolis, I want to look at your work computers. All your personal technology contained a virus."

"A virus? I have virus protection. You put that on too."

"A year ago. Technology moves faster than most companies can keep up."

"Boarding first class to Orlando," came from the speakers.

"What did the virus do?"

"I sent the information to Ben. He can figure out anything. It could be harmless." He stood and offered me his hand.

For a second, I stared at it and finally laid my hand in his. "Or?"

"I'd rather not discuss hypotheticals."

That didn't help my anxiety.

What would anyone gain by bugging my personal technology?

As the airline employee scanned my ticket, I knew the answer. They could learn everything about me.

Dani

A few hours later, Eli walked with me into the rehab facility, his suspicious gaze scanning everything and everyone around us. After taking the elevator to the second floor, Eli entered a code into a box near security doors—a code I could only assume came from Jack, Mom's bodyguard. The doors opened. Jack stood from the chair beside the closed door to Mom's new room. "Dr. Sinclair. Mr. Rhodes."

"Mr. Webb," Eli replied.

"How is she doing?" I asked.

"The move over here from the hospital wore her out." Jack tipped his chin toward the door. "She'll be happy to see you."

My gaze went to Eli's.

Was I silently asking permission?

Before I could continue that thought, he questioned Jack.

"Is there anyone else in there with her?"

"No. We're hoping she'll get some rest."

"I'll wait out here," Eli said, in his way of giving me permission to enter without him.

Squaring my shoulders, I decided that this pecking order was a subject for another time. With a nod, I opened the door. With her eyes closed and her body beneath the covers, my mother looked small, almost childlike, lying in the hospital-style bed. Next to her bed, I noticed a walker.

Spinning slowly, I took in the room. It was a little larger than her room had been back at the hospital and there was a large window, currently covered by blinds. Maybe I should go to her home and bring a few things to make this space more personalized and less sterile.

"Dani. Oh, you're here."

I turned with a grin and walked toward the bed. "Hey, Mom. How are you feeling?"

She wiggled in the bed and pushed a button at the side that lifted her to a sitting position. "Physically, I'm better." She pointed at the walker. "They're letting me get out of bed as long as I promise to use that thing."

Tears glistened in her eyes as she swallowed. "I

know we spoke on the phone but tell me again. How was the service?"

"Sad," I answered truthfully. "Everyone is shocked."

"I still can't believe it's all true." She wiped a tear from her cheek. "I don't know how to live without your father."

Moving beyond the rail, I sat on the edge of her bed and laid my hand on her blanket-covered legs. "The way Dad would want you to live. Not giving up."

"Damien is trying to talk me into moving back to Carmel, even offered for me to stay with him, Ella, and Dylan."

A smile teased my lips. "He told me. He wants me to encourage it."

She shrugged.

"Oh, it sounds fun."

"I've been thinking about it." She sighed. "I would love to spend time with Dylan, but I'm also not ready to give up my independence. Maybe I could travel back and forth. Our home here will seem too lonely without Derek." She feigned a smile. "I'll be expecting him to walk through the door."

I remembered my brother's other request. "Damien wants me to FaceTime him." I touched his number in my contacts. As soon as he answered, I handed the phone to Mom. While they spoke, I wandered around the room, looking in the closet and drawers. Opening the blinds, I let the natural light stream through the window, while seeing the palm trees from the second floor.

When she hung up, she said, "He wants you to call him later."

Exhaling, I nodded. "Do you want me to get you some things from your house?"

"That would be wonderful. I made a list for Jack, but he won't leave me until his replacement arrives." A pink hue came to her cheeks. "And I feel better asking you to bring me panties."

"Let me get the list from Jack, and I'll bring the things to you tonight." I exhaled. "What are they saying? How long will you be here?"

Mom shook her head. "Too long, if you ask me. There's already been one physical therapist in here to do an evaluation. There's a lot of red tape."

"I can only stay for a few days, but Damien, Ella, and I will take turns coming down to be with you."

"That's silly. If you can get my things from home, I'll be fine here." She glanced toward the window. "Originally, they had me on the ground floor, but Jack intervened. He said the second floor was safer. Apparently, the glass isn't bulletproof." She laid her head back. "I can't believe this is my life."

"I'm sorry, Mom. It's all of our lives right now. Until we find the man who shot Dad and learn his motivation, we are all potentially targets."

"Do you have a guard with you? I don't want you traveling alone."

"I'm not alone. Eli Rhodes has taken me as an assignment."

She tilted her head. "I remember that name. Wasn't he with you during the Darius debacle?"

With me.

"Yes."

"Oh, that's nice to have someone you're familiar with. Mr. Clark, the man in charge of Guardian Security, asked me if I would like to have Jack replaced, after…" She inhaled. "I said if he wanted to stay, I wanted him. I don't blame Jack for what happened. It occurred so fast. I guess I didn't want to lose both your dad and Jack. I need some familiarity."

Familiarity.

"I feel safe with Eli. I know he'll do whatever he can." The problem was I wanted more than the professional relationship. I wanted more than a temporary assignment.

My wants didn't matter.

"Honey," Mom said, "they'll find the horrible man, and then we'll find our new normal."

I nodded. "You're right." I squeezed her leg. "It's good to see you doing better. The last time we were down here, there were concerns about your mobility." I forced a smile. "Now look at you." I pointed to the walker. "You're going to be racing soon."

"I don't know about racing. I'm happy to be walking."

Eli and I were quiet on the elevator ride down to the first floor. It was as we approached the front of the building that the crowd of people beyond the glass entry came into view. Eli reached for my arm.

"What do you think it's about?" I asked.

The muscles pulled tight in his cheeks. "I don't like it." He walked us to the front desk and spoke to the woman manning the door and phones. "What is going on out there?"

The overly bleached-blond-haired woman wearing a t-shirt with the name of the facility, looked up and scanned Eli before pressing her red-painted lips together. "They're reporters."

"Why are there reporters?"

"Patient confidentiality. I can't say."

I gasped. "Is this about my mother?"

She narrowed her gaze at me. "And you are...?"

"Dr. Sinclair," Eli answered. "She has joint POA for her mother, Mrs. Marsha Sinclair. Are those reporters here about Mrs. Sinclair?"

"I'm not supposed to say." Her forehead furrowed as she returned her gaze to me. "Yes, they are. News got out that she was transferred here. You don't need to worry. Our security forbade them from entering the facility."

Eli looked around. "Is there a back door accessible by car?"

"Yes. However, it's only for the use of employees."

"Where is it?" he asked.

After a moment's hesitation, the woman pointed down the hallway with the elevators. "Turn left at the end of that hallway."

Eli again seized my arm and tugged me away from the front desk. "Go back there. I'll bring the car around."

My pulse kicked up a few notches. "You're going to leave me here?"

"I'm not leaving you. I'm avoiding those assholes out there." His gaze went to my purse, wordlessly reminding me of the pepper spray within. "Stay vigilant. I'll pull the car around back."

The thought of being alone was suddenly terrifying. I shook my head. "They're just reporters. I won't comment."

Clenching his jaw, Eli lowered his tone. "Dani, if reporters know your mother and you are here, then the perp could too. I'm not walking you out the front door."

The perp.

Dad was shot only miles away.

Swallowing my growing fear, I nodded. "Okay. I'll meet you at the back door."

"Don't exit the building until you see the car."

Again, I nodded.

My pulse thumped in my ears as I watched Eli open and walk beyond the glass doors. Some of the reporters began shouting questions. Even if I strained, I couldn't make out what they were asking.

Opening my purse, I found the small canister of pepper spray. I twisted the lock as Eli had shown me. My hand trembled as I recalled him also telling me to aim for an attacker's eyes. With the canister in my grasp, I walked the direction the woman had indicated, down the hallway toward the dining area. All the tables were empty in anticipation of the evening meal.

Mom told me she would be eating in her room.

Turning left, I continued walking until I reached the door with the word *Exit* above the jamb. Through the window, I saw multiple cars. No doubt this was the employee parking area.

A woman in scrubs appeared from behind a door.

Startled, I jumped.

CHAPTER

EIGHT

Dani

The woman in scrubs sized me up and down. "Ma'am, this is the employee exit. You'll need to go through the front and sign out."

I forced a smile and read her name tag. "I know this is unusual, Becky. My ride is picking me up here."

The downturn of her pressed-together lips displayed her obvious annoyance. "For the safety of our patients, our protocol—"

Eli pulled up to the curb driving the black SUV that Guardian Security lent him.

Without another word, I pushed the bar, unlatching the door. For a split second, I anticipated alarms. There were none as I hurried down the sidewalk to the SUV. The woman called something after me, but I had no intention of responding.

Eli rushed from the driver's seat and opened the back door. As he shut the door, he waved to the concerned woman. Once he was back behind the steering wheel, he exhaled. His green stare met mine in the rearview mirror. "Did you have any problems?"

"Just that employee. Her name tag said Becky. It should have been Karen. She's probably reporting me as we speak." I twisted the top of the cylinder still in my grasp to lock and pushed the pepper spray back into my purse. When I looked up, Eli was turned toward me with a smile. "What?"

"Good girl."

I lifted my eyebrows.

"The pepper spray. I hoped you'd have it at the ready."

"Yeah, Becky almost got a taste."

Eli chuckled as he turned the SUV around.

"Tell me about the reporters," I said.

"They're fishing for information. I didn't say a word to them."

"Did any of them look suspicious?" I asked. "Was it overkill to whisk me out the back door?"

"At this moment, nothing is overkill," Eli said as he steered the SUV around to the front driveway of the rehab facility. The grounds near the front doors were still filled with people with microphones. I saw a TV crew from WFTV News 9 filming. "I don't trust any of them."

My pulse kicked up as I briefly scanned the crowd. "I hate living like this."

"You can hate it, Dani." His sunglass-shielded stare shifted to the rearview mirror. "You just need to keep living."

I laid my head back against the seat, trying to make sense of my thoughts as Eli navigated the Florida area traffic. Within the Villages, the large black SUV stood out among the vast number of golf carts as we pulled up to Mom's villa.

Once we were parked in Mom's driveway, Eli spoke, "Let me do an inside sweep, and then I'll come to get you."

My nostrils flared as I nodded. In only a few weeks, I'd grown fatigued of the routine that showed no signs of stopping soon. When Eli got out of the driver's seat, he left the engine and air conditioning running.

I watched as Eli entered the villa. A short time later, he returned, turned off the vehicle, and escorted me to the front door.

Inside, the absence of my father caused my steps to stutter.

"Dani?"

I inhaled, refusing to discuss my feelings. "I'm fine. Let me look for the things on Mom's list."

He pressed his lips together and nodded.

While I searched to fulfill Mom's requests, Eli walked room to room, surveying every outlet, corner, and picture frame. Next, he sat down at their computer and inserted the same thumb drive he had on my laptop. I filled a beach bag with various items, opening drawers and going through their closet.

The sight of Dad's clothes within their closet returned the lump to my throat. His golf bag was next to Mom's in the garage along with their bikes and golf cart. Running my finger over the bicycle handlebars, I remembered how hard Dad had worked to regain his health after his heart attacks. It was then that I thought about their dog.

I hurried back into the house. "I should go next door and check on Hoosier."

Eli's gaze went from the computer screen to me. "What's a Hoosier?"

"A person from Indiana. It's also the name of Mom and Dad's dog." The villa seems too empty without Mom, Dad, and that little dog."

"You said the dog's next door?"

"When we came down right after the shooting, I made arrangements with Carol next door. She was happy to help." I narrowed my eyes at Eli who was scanning the monitor of my parents' computer. "You don't think Jack or any of the other people assigned to this case would have already checked their electronics?"

His lips quirked up in a lopsided grin. "I prefer to do things myself. That way I know they're done right."

"Did you find the same virus you found on my things?"

"According to Ben, it was already found."

"While we're alone... tell me what it does?"

He shook his head.

"Why?"

Instead of answering, he looked at the beach bag. "Do you have everything your mom requested?"

I lifted the bag. "I do."

"What do you want to do tonight?"

"Besides get some straight answers from you?"

His smirk was back. "Besides that."

"If my laptop passed your inspection, I guess we'll take these things to Mom and then go to the villa you rented. I can catch up on emails and find out if I'm missing anything important happening at Sinclair."

"No live music or partying in the Villages?"

"If I said yes, you'd tell me it wasn't safe."

Eli removed his thumb drive from my parents' computer. "Sounds like you remember things about me, too."

"Not *you* particularly," I lied. "I've had a few other bodyguards, and you're all the same."

He took a step closer, the musky notes of his cologne tickling my nose and his massive chest settling at my eye level. His tenor dropped an octave. "We're *all* the same."

That wasn't true.

Melinda didn't cause my core to twist or my nipples to bead. Even Silas Hartman, the other man who worked with Ella and me a year ago, didn't have the same effect on my body that Eli did. I swallowed and looked up. "Yes. All very predictable."

For longer than necessary, we stood merely inches

apart as his strikingly green gaze stared down at me, penetrating my veneer and searching deep into my heart and soul. Maintaining eye contact, I stared back, determined not to be the first to blink. My decision to remain resolute in keeping our relationship professional grew more difficult to remember as my breathing shallowed.

Finally, his deep baritone timbre shattered the stare-down. "You're not a convincing liar." He winked. "Don't play poker."

"I'll have you know, I'm excellent at Texas Hold'em."

"I'll walk with you to the neighbors."

The neighbors?

"Hoosier," Eli reminded.

"Right." Our face-off had my mind a bit preoccupied. I tried to move on, rambling on about things I may have already told him. "The neighbor's name is Carol. She's a widow who moved in about the same time as Mom and Dad..." We locked Mom's place and walked along the sidewalk to Carol's house. As soon as I rang the doorbell, I heard the familiar bark.

"Dani," Carol said as she opened the door, allowing Hoosier to rush out and greet me.

I picked him up and nuzzled my face against his soft light-brown fur. "Thank you for keeping him."

"Come in," she waved as she looked up at Eli.

Once in the foyer of her lovely villa, I spoke to Carol, "This is Eli. And this is Carol," I introduced to Eli.

"May I get the two of you anything to drink?"

"We can't stay. I just wanted to check on Hoosier. Mom will be happy to hear he's doing well."

"How is Marsha doing?"

"She's up and walking with a walker. And if I know my mom, she won't need that for too long." I lowered Hoosier to the tile floor. "Can I give you any money for his food and care?"

Carol waved her hand. "There was plenty of food in the garage. If I need to buy more, I will." She grinned. "I'm enjoying his company."

"Have you been in the Sinclairs' home?" Eli asked.

"Yes, we exchanged keys long ago." Her eyes widened. "Is that a problem?" She covered her lips with her fingertips. "There was no tape. It's not considered a crime scene, is it?"

"No," he replied. "Have you noticed anyone else coming and going?"

"Right after the...what happened, there were people there for days. I spoke to one man who said he was a detective."

"Did he have a badge?" I asked.

"Oh goodness. I can't remember."

"Did he say which department he represented?"

Carol scrunched her nose. "I'm sorry. I didn't ask."

"Anyone else?"

She nodded. "Last Tuesday, there was a group of people. No, it was Wednesday, because I play pickle-ball on Wednesdays."

"People?" I encouraged.

"Yes, they were there when I got home, carrying boxes from Marsha's house."

"What was in the boxes?" Eli asked.

She shook her head. "Papers, I think. They were file-like boxes. I couldn't really see what all they had."

I tried to understand. "Boxes of papers?"

Carol nodded. "Papers or small books. I was going to ask who they were, but they seemed very no-nonsense." She wrapped her arms around herself. "Gave off a vibe." She looked at Eli and back to me. "Some people do."

I grinned. I supposed Eli gave off a vibe too.

Carol went on, "I did notice that they were wearing rubber gloves and dark uniforms."

My gaze went back to Eli. "I want to look closer in Dad's office." I reached out to Carol, touching her hand. "Thank you. You have my number. If you see anyone else or need anything, please reach out to me."

She lowered her arms. "Give Marsha my love."

I nodded as we walked toward the front door and paused to give Hoosier one more pet. "I will. Thank you."

Once we were back outside, I asked, "Was anyone at Guardian aware that someone took items from their house?"

"I'm going to find out."

Standing on Mom's front porch, I asked, "What were you looking for earlier? Do you think this house was bugged?"

"We can talk about that in a more secure location." He unlocked the door.

If it was possible, the house seemed even quieter than it had been a few minutes earlier. I went straight into the front office, separated from the foyer by a set of French glass doors. Upon opening the doors, I was hit with the familiar scent of my father. It wasn't anything in particular, just a reminder that this was where he spent his time.

I started to reach for a drawer handle and stopped. "Should we try to get fingerprints?"

"Carol said they wore gloves, but let's be sure." He reached into his suitcoat pocket and pulled out latex gloves. "Here. Put these on."

I quirked my eyebrow. "You just carry these with you?"

"I'm prepared."

Slipping my hands into the gloves, I began opening the drawers to Dad's desk. Eli also donned gloves and began to inspect the tall bookcases. The top drawer contained pens, paper clips, a stapler, checkbooks, and a calculator. The last item made me smile. Only my parents would still have a calculator when their phones were capable of everything. The next drawer had stacks of notepads and envelopes. I opened the larger file drawer and gasped.

"It's completely empty."

My hands started to tremble as Eli came closer and looked down into the cavernous space. "Do you have any idea what he kept in there?"

"No." I had a thought. "There's something else. Dad showed me this after he had it installed." I stood. Going to the large window that faced the street, I closed the plantation shades, dimming the room. After I turned on the light, I looked at the opposite wall. The bookcases Eli had been inspecting went from the floor to the ceiling on each side. In the middle was a cabinet with a decanter of bourbon. Above the cabinet was a large, framed picture of Sinclair Pharmaceuticals. Pulling on the corner of the frame, the picture swung out, revealing a safe. "He thought it was very Hollywood."

"Who knew about it?"

I shrugged. "Knowing Dad, he probably told anyone who would listen."

"Do you know the combination?"

I stared at the digital keypad. "I could make some educated guesses." My gaze met Eli's. "It's not going to explode if I enter the wrong code, is it?"

He ran his hands around the edges. "Hard to say for sure. I don't see or feel any wiring, but then again…" His lips quirked as he took a picture of the keypad. "It's more likely to lock if the wrong code is entered too many times. In that case the emergency key would be needed."

"I could message Mom. If Dad had any important documents, he wouldn't have left them in his desk. They'd be in that safe."

Eli sent the picture of the front of the safe to the Guardian Security team, to learn the number of digits that would be needed. At the same time, I called Mom's cell phone. It rang three times before going to her voicemail.

"No answer," I told him. "Hopefully, she's asleep. We could take her things to her and ask her for the combination or where the key would be. Then we could come back."

Eli nodded. "I want to talk to Jack. Find out if he knows anything about the people coming and going." He pushed the picture back against the wall.

The façade was well hung. If they didn't know that it was hiding a safe, no one would be the wiser. The problem was that my father was a sharer. I imagined him standing in here with golf buddies, drinking bourbon, and showing them all his hidden safe.

As we turned to leave, the doorbell rang.

CHAPTER
NINE

Eli

"It's probably Carol or one of the other neighbors," Dani said, walking past me.

I reached for her arm. "Stay back. I'll answer it." Unlocking the safety on my gun, I kept it low to my side as I entered the foyer and looked through the side window. "Fuck."

"What?" Despite my instructions to stay back, Dani was now at my side.

"County Sheriff's Department."

A loud knock preceded the sound of a deep voice. "Open up. Sumter County Sheriff's Department."

I holstered the gun I'd gotten from my Guardian contact, Mitchell Gray. Lowering my voice, I whispered, "Answer their questions, but don't volunteer any information."

"Maybe they're here to tell us they found the shooter or know who took Dad's things."

Doubtful. If they were coming to share, they wouldn't be banging on the door.

Turning the deadbolt, I opened the door and met the stare of two men in uniform. "Deputies, how can we help you?"

One spoke while the other tried to look around me. "This address is under surveillance due to a recent crime. Explain who you are and why you're in the residence."

Dani pushed forward and offered her hand. "I'm Dr. Danielle Sinclair. My parents...my mother," she rephrased, "lives here. We were getting her a few personal items for her stay in physical therapy rehab."

"Do you have ID, Dr. Sinclair?"

"Yes. Let me get my purse."

As she walked away, the second officer looked me up and down. "And you are?"

"I'm Dr. Sinclair's private security."

"Can you verify that?"

Dani came back with her driver's license in her hand and passed it to the officer she'd spoken with. "This is Elijah Rhodes. He works with Guardian Security. After what happened to my father..."

The deputy handed her back her ID. "Dr. Sinclair, your address is Carmel, Indiana. Are you visiting or are you staying here? Will you be in and out of the home?"

I replied. "That depends on her mother. You can understand what a strain the family is under."

"I appreciate you watching the house," Dani said. "Have you been keeping an eye on it since my father...?"

"The case has gotten the media's attention," the deputy said. "People nowadays can find addresses with a few clicks on their keypad. We're trying to avoid crimes of opportunity."

"Thank you," she said. "Have you had any other calls about anyone coming around the house?"

"Not on our watch."

I stepped forward. "It's good to know which department to contact if there are any questions. Your detectives should have Dr. Sinclair and her brother Damien Sinclair's contact information."

Dani feigned a smile. "We hope that soon you'll have a lead on who killed our father."

"Yes, ma'am, we're working on that." He nodded. "Our condolences."

"Thank you."

After an awkward moment, the two turned and walked down the sidewalk toward their car.

Dani exhaled.

I stood for a moment with my hand on the doorknob, staring out toward the street. I had a thought. Camera doorbells were no longer the exception. "Are you ready to go?"

"That visit was odd, if you ask me."

I couldn't agree more.

Locking the door behind us, I walked Dani to the SUV. The sheriff's marked vehicle was still parked on the street. "We're being watched."

"If they are watching the house that closely, maybe it was their department that took Dad's files."

"I had another idea."

As I drove us back to the rehab center, Dani brought up her earlier question. "The way you were looking around when we first arrived, did you expect to find cameras or microphones?"

"No."

"You don't lie well either. You're saying you were simply fascinated with my parents' outlets. They truly are top of the line. You see, they provide electricity. So unique."

I shook my head, slipping on my sunglasses. "I didn't expect to find any because they were already found. If I had found any, that would mean either someone from Guardian missed one, which is unacceptable, or it could mean that someone else installed new ones."

Dani leaned forward. "You're saying that my parents' home was bugged?"

"They'd been employing Guardian for over a year. The cameras were ours."

"Did Mom and Dad know?"

"They signed the contract for our security. The exact locations and number of cameras weren't common knowledge. Don't discuss it with anyone."

"Does Damien know?" she asked.

"Not to my knowledge."

"What's the purpose of keeping that information from him?"

"Who benefits from your father's death?"

"No one." Her answer came without hesitation. "Damien accused Darius of involvement, but even that doesn't make sense. Darius isn't on Sinclair's executive board. His only connection is that he owns shares of Sinclair stock that allow him information and bonuses. None of that would increase with Dad's death." She gave it more thought. "Dad's will was updated after his health scare. Everything he owns, money and property, reverts to Mom. Even Damien and I don't receive anything until Mom is gone."

"She was shot."

In the rearview mirror, I watched as Dani pressed her fingers against her temples. "Don't do that, Eli. Don't make me suspect my own brother. Damien wouldn't do such a thing."

Making her suspect her brother wasn't my goal. However, I wanted her to understand the multitude of possibilities. "I didn't say that he did." I turned the SUV into the driveway of the rehab facility. The number of people outside the front door had decreased, yet there were still about half a dozen. "I'm driving you around to the back. We'll park there and instead of taking the elevator, we can take back stairs."

"There are back stairs. How did you learn about those?"

"I texted Jack while you were looking for your mother's things."

"How will we get through a locked door?"

I parked the SUV and pulled out my phone. "Jack will be down in less than a minute."

"What about Mom?"

"She's inside her room."

Dani had her lower lip tugged between her teeth as I sent Jack a text telling him we were here.

When I opened her door, she stood, beach bag in hand and looked up at me, her navy eyes again covered by sunglasses. "I don't like feeling that I need to ask your permission to enter a room—like my mother's."

"Don't think of it like that."

"How should I think of it?"

Placing my hand in the small of her back, I willed myself not to think about the physical connection as I guided her toward the door. "Think of it as staying safe."

My touch was only a brief contact, yet the familiarity I felt with her was wrong. The longing I tried to suppress to once again feel my lips on hers was also wrong.

The door Dani had exited earlier in the day opened as we approached. Jack Webb was on the other side. As we came closer, he handed me a key. Next time, I'd be able to get us in and out of this door without taking him away from his assignment.

"Is that a key to this door?" Dani asked as she pushed her sunglasses to the top of her head.

"Yes, ma'am."

As we stepped into the hallway, Dani pointed to our left. "That was where Becky came from."

"The staircase is through this door," Jack said, opening the barrier on the right. Our footsteps echoed on the metal steps within the cement-enclosed stairway. The door on the second floor opened without an issue. We followed Jack as we made our way to Mrs. Sinclair's room.

"The staircase must be within security," Dani whispered. When I met her gaze, she added, "We didn't have to enter a code."

"The staff uses it," Jack said.

"If they do..." she said.

"Anyone could," I finished.

As we turned the corner near Marsha's room, my pulse quickened. Her door was open. A quick glance at Dani and we both took off running.

"Mom," she called.

Marsha's bed was empty.

CHAPTER

TEN

Dani

I rushed to the attached bathroom, calling for my mother. The room was empty. With my body quaking, I made a mental inventory of what I'd seen during my earlier visit. "Her walker is gone." I turned to Jack. "Was she in here when you came to us?"

"Yes," he said as he rushed from the room.

Eli and I followed as Jack made his way to the nurses' station. While we couldn't hear his words, as his body visibly relaxed, our steps slowed.

Jack turned to us. "A nurse's aide came and took her to physical therapy."

Eli and I were now close to the desk. I turned to the

woman in scrubs. My heart sank as I read her name tag for the second time in the same day.

Becky feigned a smile. "It's you."

I tried for my nicest tone. "Where is physical therapy?"

"I'm sorry, miss. Only patients are allowed to access the therapy room. You see there can be multiple patients receiving treatment at the same time. It's for our patients' privacy."

Inhaling, I straightened my shoulders. "Becky, my father was murdered. My mother was also shot. At no time is she to be without a member of her security team."

"We have rules."

"Mr. Webb stepped away for only a moment. The three of us will go to where she is. Once we're certain of her safety, Mr. Webb will remain outside the room. If that isn't in her chart, put it in there. My mother's life could be in danger." I didn't let her reply. "I will ask you once again. Where is physical therapy?"

"Ms. Sinclair—"

"Doctor," I said, correcting her. "My name is Dr. Sinclair. If you don't understand a matter of security, we will have my mother transferred to a more competent facility."

Becky picked up a telephone from the desk and pushed a few buttons. I imagined that she was calling security to have us thrown out.

"Todd," she said, still giving me the side-eye. "This

is Becky on two. Did Gina retrieve the patient from 215 down to you for her physical therapy evaluation?" She nodded. "Yes, Marsha Sinclair. Thank you." Her eyes met mine. "Mrs. Sinclair's security will be down in a few minutes. I explained that they are to remain outside the treatment room. A Mr. Webb will wait at the door." She nodded again. "Thank you." As she hung up the phone receiver, she stood straighter. "First floor, west wing. There are signs to the physical therapy department. Todd, one of our therapists, is expecting you."

I managed to thank her as the three of us made our way toward the elevators.

Once we were inside, Eli whispered, "There's the feisty assignment I remember."

His comment released a bit of the tension growing between my shoulder blades. "I should have reached for the pepper spray."

On the first floor, we made our way down a long hallway, past the entry, and past the dining area. Signs pointed to the direction of physical therapy. There was a man in scrubs waiting for us at the door.

"I'm Todd. Mr. Webb?" he asked.

"I'm Mr. Webb," Jack said, "Mrs. Sinclair's security."

I stepped forward. "Todd, I'd like to see my mother."

He reached for the door handle. "No other patients are in therapy right now. You may all come in."

A gust of breath came from my lungs at the sight of

my mother. She was sitting on a contraption, moving her arms and her legs and talking to a woman in scrubs. "Mom."

"Dani." Her eyes widened. "Everyone is here."

I went closer. "Mom, you shouldn't be transported from one place to another without Jack or another member of your detail."

"I'm sorry, Mrs. Sinclair," Jack said. "I shouldn't have stepped away."

Mom leaned back, stopping her motion. "Jack, I'm fine. They said it wouldn't be long. They're still evaluating me."

I leaned over and kissed her cheek. "You scared me."

"I'm sorry, dear."

I looked at the woman with her. "Could I speak to her for a moment?"

The therapist looked as if she were about to argue and wisely decided against it. Briefly, I wondered if Becky had called this department again after we stepped away and warned them about me.

I lowered my voice. "Mom, do you know the combination to Dad's safe?"

She closed her eyes. "Yes, it's 1983."

A smile curled my lips. "The year you were married."

"Yes." Her brow furrowed. "What do you need from there?"

Not wanting to tell her about the missing papers, I came up with a reason. "We're looking for his insurance policies. We couldn't find them in the desk."

"Oh, you wouldn't. Your father kept his journals, the ones from his and your grandfather's time at Sinclair Pharmaceuticals, in his desk. I would often find him sitting in there and rereading your grandfather's notes and scribbling in the margins."

She had my attention. "What kind of notes?"

"You could look at them. There were notes about the company and different strategies they had. There were some about the original formulas and speculations on ones Sinclair never chose to manufacture." She shook her head. "All outdated, I'm sure."

"Had Dad ever showed them to Damien?"

"Excuse me," the therapist said. "We only have a few more minutes."

The large clock on the wall read 5:15.

I took a step back. "Mom, call me if you need me. I dropped the things you wanted in your room. Eli and I are going to head back to your house and then to the villa he rented. I have some work."

"Are you leaving tomorrow?"

"No. I'll be here until Sunday."

Her smile returned. "It's good to know you're close. After this, they're supposed to bring me my dinner."

"Mrs. Sinclair..."

Backing away, I watched Mom resume her therapy. I met up with Eli and Jack in the hallway. The two were talking.

"Guardian's cameras were taken out of the house the day after the shooting," Jack said. "Ben didn't want them discovered by other investigators."

That accounted for some of the people Carol saw.

Eli pressed his lips together. "According to the neighbor, there were many different people in and out shortly after the shooting. The curious thing is what else she told us. Last..." He looked at me. "Wednesday?"

I nodded.

"Last Wednesday, two days ago, a team of people in dark clothes removed boxes of papers from the house."

Jack shook his head. "Our interior cameras are gone, but I've been watching the outdoor ones. I didn't receive a notification."

"Did you receive one this afternoon?" Eli asked. "We were there."

Jack pulled out his phone. "No."

Eli inhaled. "We'll get that fixed."

"According to Carol," I said, "it would have happened on Wednesday morning. She remembered because she said she saw the people when she came home from pickleball."

"Send me the link to access the doorbell and back-yard cameras," Eli said. "I've got an idea to access other cameras in the neighborhood. Let's see who we're dealing with."

"Why would law enforcement disable or block the doorbell camera?" I asked.

Both men turned my direction. "It happens some-times if they expect to conduct an interview. They can scramble the signal, so it isn't recorded."

"But no one was there." I thought about the time-line. "It was the day before the funeral. It could be assumed that we'd all be in Indianapolis."

They both nodded.

Eli spoke, "Law enforcement aren't the only ones with the technology to scramble video feed."

A cold chill peppered my flesh.

"Did your mother tell you the combination?" Eli asked.

"She did." I turned to Jack. "Were you aware of Dad's safe in his office?"

"Yes, ma'am. He never shared his combination. Told me that all men deserved to protect their secrets."

I scrunched my nose. "My father said that? He had secrets to protect."

"That's a direct quote."

"How about his old journals, the ones in his desk?"

"What about them?" Jack asked.

"Did you ever read them?"

He shook his head. "I know for a fact they weren't all in his desk. There were some in his safe as well."

My gaze met Eli's. "Let's go check it out."

As we turned, Eli's hand went into the small of my back.

The more he touched me, the greater my craving for him increased. It wasn't just the way he wordlessly directed me. It was an overwhelming sense of safety I felt when he was near. Whether it was the warmth of his hand, the scent of his cologne, or the sound of his deep voice, they all had a calming effect.

On our drive back to Mom's house, I told Eli what Mom said about Dad's old journals. "Why would anyone want old journals. My grandfather's notes would need to have been written over fifty years ago."

While he was listening and nodding, Eli was unusually quiet.

"What are you thinking about?"

He exhaled. "I want to do some research. If Guardian has me set up with the needed technology, I should be able to access not only your parents' cameras, but also those of their neighbors. Once I find out what time Carol plays pickleball on Wednesdays, I'll have the timeline for when the people came to take the journals and whatever else they took."

"Should we ask the county sheriff's department if they were the ones who did it?"

Eli shook his head. "If they didn't, they'll want to open an investigation. I'd rather do my own investigation." He hesitated. "Dani, I don't want to frighten you any more than you already are." His sunglass-covered gaze went to the rearview mirror. "It was good to hear your determination when speaking to Becky."

"Well, she's had it in for me ever since I went through that door. I sure as hell wasn't going to let her stop me from making sure Mom was safe."

His lips curled in a smile.

Even though I couldn't see his green eyes beneath

the sunglasses, I somehow felt them even through the mirror. Or maybe it was wishful thinking.

"I'm concerned about what we may find," he said.

"What secrets did my dad have?"

Eli pulled the SUV onto the driveway. "We're about to find out."

CHAPTER

ELEVEN

Dani

The descending sun sent long shadows over my mother's lush green lawn. After Eli did an obligatory sweep of the home, we entered together, immediately going to Dad's office. The closed blinds gave an eerie feel, peppering my arms with goose bumps. Flipping the light switch did little to relieve the sensation.

The office flooded with light.

Neither of us spoke as Eli pulled the picture away from the safe door. Before I could enter the combination, Eli reached for my arm. "Maybe I should do this alone."

I looked up at him. "Why?"

"Because we don't know what we'll find. What if

there's something that could sour your memories of your father."

I inhaled. "Eli, you're here to protect me from harm, not to protect my emotions. I want to know what Dad considered safe-worthy. Besides, my father was a great man. If he had secrets, maybe those will point us toward his killer."

"We also could find nothing."

"Are you suggesting that the people who took his journals also broke into his safe?" I asked.

"I just mean, that assuming there are objects or whatever inside there...it could be that none of what we find is significant."

"Then we know."

He reached for my shoulders. "I don't want to see you disappointed."

For a moment, I stared into his emerald-green eyes, searching for an answer to his sudden trepidation. His orbs filled with swirls of gold, keeping his thoughts as hidden as his recent answers. "Again, I want to do this."

He swallowed, his Adam's apple bobbing as he closed his eyes and opened them. "I need to know you're safe." He tilted his head forward and lowered his chin to my hair. "Dani, let me open it."

I closed my eyes, feeling his warm breath on my hair and the strength in his hold. Without warning, I moved back and pushed up to my tiptoes, bringing my lips to his. Eli's hands moved to my cheeks as the kiss deepened, taking away my anxiousness as well as my breath.

"Dani."

My name resonated through the office like a low growl.

Pulling away, I pressed my tingling lips together and shook my head. "I did that. You said that you shouldn't have kissed me—before. This time, I kissed you. Decide what you're going to do. Either you'll stay and see this through, or you'll leave me like you did last time." I turned toward the safe.

Eli spun me until we were face-to-face. "I'm not fucking leaving."

"I know you want to protect me. I get that. What I need to know is that you'll not run."

He ran his palms up and down my arms. "I won't run. The problem is, I want more than a kiss, more than your warm, sweet lips, and that's wrong."

"Says who?"

"It's not only Ben's policy, but my own." He shook his head. "Connections blur lines that should stay distinct."

"Then stop working on my assignment."

"What?" he asked, confused.

"I want you, too." I swallowed. "I'm a consenting adult, Eli. I want whatever we can get. Let someone else have my case. If what's between us only lasts for a short time, then at least we can say we had that. If it's meant to be longer—"

He touched my lips with his finger. "I can't drop you as my assignment."

My neck stiffened. "You're saying that you'd rather have this job than see where the two of us could go?"

"Fuck no. I want you. That want is selfish." He pressed his firm lips together. "Keeping you safe is more than a job. I feel the need to protect you deep inside my bones, an unrelenting demand to ensure your safety. That outcome is more important than a physical desire."

I swallowed, fighting the burning in my eyes. I'd laid my feelings on the line and been rejected. My voice cooled to a frigid tone as I reached for the safe keypad. "Fine, Eli. Do your job."

Before I could press the first button, Eli seized my shoulders and spun my body until my back was against the tall bookcase. The shelves pressed into my back and the hardness of Eli's body pushed against my front.

Gasping for breath, I stared upward into the cyclone of gold flecks spinning in his green irises. "What the hell?"

His lips crashed down on mine as they had the year before, bruising and taking. The rush of adrenaline flooding my circulation caused an ensuing cataclysmic eruption of my emotions. As much as I wanted what he was doing, I fought with all my might, pushing back against his solid, unmoving chest and twisting my face from side to side.

Relentless, Eli released my shoulders and palmed

both sides of my cheeks, holding my face in place as he continued his kiss. Synapse after synapse exploded; sparks ignited. This was more than a kiss. It was an exorcism.

The flood of endorphins ripped at my grief, my sadness, intertwining desire and reminding me of my loneliness. Despite the devotion to my work and the support of my family, I had a void within me, one exemplified by the loss of my father.

Connection.

A real connection was what was missing from my life. The desire was so intense that I'd refused to face it, to acknowledge that deficit when Eli left a year ago. While I couldn't face it then, at this moment, I had no choice.

The physical manifestation of my desire had me pinned against the bookshelf in my father's office.

With my heart thumping violently against my breastbone, my body stopped struggling. Buzzing filled my ears as Eli's tongue danced with mine and my thoughts collided, turning rational notions into molten goo.

My father.

Danger.

Eli's rejection.

My kiss.

His passion.

Him.

Pressing my breasts against his solid chest, I savored the taste of his lips and the sensation of his tongue. With the hunger of a starving man, Eli continued his devouring of my lips. His hands lowered, pulling my hips to him. Our closeness did more than bruise my lips. My nipples hardened and my pussy twisted.

Finally, but too soon, Eli released his hold, leaning back while keeping our hips connected. He tipped his forehead to the top of my head. "I'm..."

The fire he'd not only lit, but tended, morphed from desire to anger. My volume rose. "Don't you dare apologize." I reached up to his face as he'd done to mine. My gaze locked on his.

He cocked his face to the side as he wiped a tear from my cheek that I didn't realize I'd released. His deep tenor slowed as his emerald eyes held me in place. "I'm not sorry for the kiss or the way I feel about you." He swallowed. "I'm sorry if what I feel interferes with keeping you safe. I could never live with myself." He caressed my cheek. "I don't want to be on the earth if you're not on it too."

"What about Ben's rules? What about yours?"

Eli shook his head. "For now, I'm not going to worry about those." His nostrils flared as his green eyes sparkled. "I knew coming back to you was a mistake."

When I tried to move away, he held me tight.

"Not a mistake, that's the wrong word. I knew coming back would push my own boundaries. I told myself that I could keep my hands and feelings in check." His lips quirked upward. "In most instances, I'm always in control, overly so."

My tension eased as his words registered. "You're not running away?"

"No." He inhaled and took a step back. "I'm also breaking Guardian's and my own rules. But if I have to choose between this" —he grinned— "and your safety, your safety comes first."

"Don't choose." I lifted my palm to his chest. "I want you to do both."

"Fuck, Dani, I'll try."

"Okay." I lifted my hand, palm up. "Whatever we find, we find it together."

He laid his palm in mine and squeezed. "Would you consider letting me do this alone?"

I shook my head. "Not a chance."

Eli's lips quirked in a silent gesture of concession.

My pulse raced as I released his hand and turned toward the keypad. Concentrating, I entered the numbers Mom told me: 1-9-8-3 and then hit the pound sign. A green light blinked. Holding my breath, I listened as the door opened.

TWELVE

Eli

Despite her determination, as the green light flashed, I stepped in front of her, shielding her. From what, I wasn't sure. The door slowly opened, the sound of locking mechanisms moving.

"Eli," she said, pushing me. "I want to see."

I wasn't certain what I feared would be within the safe. When Jack mentioned secrets, my mind went into overdrive with possibilities.

An empty cavity.

Worse yet, documentation of...

An alternate identity.

Another family.

Proof of infidelity.

Offshore bank accounts.

Truly, the list was exhaustive.

The inside wasn't empty. The initial relief that this treasure trove hadn't been pillaged was instantaneously replaced by concern about what the contents would uncover.

"Wait," I said as Dani reached inside. "Gloves. We should have Guardian dust the items to learn if there are any fingerprints beyond your parents."

She turned to me with her beautiful swollen lips held tightly between her teeth and nodded.

I pulled two more sets of latex gloves from my suit coat pocket. Once we both had them on, we began emptying the contents. Documents, notebooks, boxes of coins, jewelry boxes, an old photo album...we didn't stop to examine anything until all of the contents were removed.

I lifted the felt liner at the bottom, revealing a large manila envelope. There was nothing written on the outside.

With the items stacked beside the bourbon decanter, Dani looked up at me. A million questions swirled through her dark blue orbs, questions I couldn't answer and those that I feared would change her world when their answers were finally discovered.

"I think we should take these things back to the rental and examine them."

Dani nodded. "I can grab another one of Mom's beach bags or I saw boxes in the garage."

"A beach bag will be less conspicuous if the sheriff's department is watching."

As she stepped away to find the beach bag, I reached for what seemed the most suspicious to me, the manila envelope. The contents were light in weight. The tab was sealed with both the sticky part and the wire prong. Next, I lifted the photo album. Opening the vinyl cover, I saw photographs neatly placed within plastic sleeves. The fashions and the yellowing of the photos told me that a number of them were old. How old was what I wanted to learn. At the sound of her approaching footsteps, I laid the album down.

"Do you think that will all fit in this one?" she asked, holding up a large blue and white striped bag with a nautical anchor on the front.

"Let's get these things packed up and get out of here."

She briefly examined each item as she placed it within the bag. "Jack said Dad mentioned he had the right to hide his secrets." Her blue stare met mine. "Do you see any obvious secrets?"

"That's not the way secrets work."

Dani sighed. "I suppose you're right."

We were minutes away from sunset as we cautiously made our way out to the SUV. I scanned the street for a marked sheriff's vehicle. There wasn't one. That didn't mean we weren't being watched.

We'd spent more time inside the villa than I'd planned. While we were both responsible for that lapse, I was determined not to allow what had happened to put Dani in the sight of danger. Continuing to scan the neighborhood, I led her to the back seat. "I know you're curious, but please wait until we can look through these things together at the villa."

With her luscious lips pressed together, Dani nodded. "Let's pick up some food and then we won't be interrupted."

That sounded good to me, but she needed to know she had options. "The Mission has three on-site restaurants. I could call for room service."

"I'm not in the mood for anything fancy."

"All right."

Dani remained unusually quiet. Each time I glanced in the rearview mirror, she was staring aimlessly out the window, watching the scenes pass by. A few minutes into our drive, her voice broke through the drone of road noise.

"Have you researched my father?"

Her question caught me off guard. "I research all my assignments."

"Recently, or last year?"

"Both," I replied honestly. "The assignment was short last year, but I did my homework. Most of my energy was focused on you, your brothers, and your sister-in-law."

"Ella?"

"Amber."

Dani scoffed. "Oh, her. I guess, technically, she was my sister-in-law, but that marriage was dissolved."

I'd learned that too, before coming back to Dani, I'd learned all I could about her family. Of course, after his murder, there was a lot of information available online and through news sources about Derek Sinclair. My research went above and beyond what they provided. "Is there something you want to know?"

She hummed. "I could assume I know all there is to know about him, but that's probably not true."

I met her gaze in the mirror. "I'd guess not. Everyone has secrets. They're not necessarily bad or ominous." I feigned a smile. "Even you, Dr. Sinclair. You have secrets."

While I'd expected her to laugh at my comment, she didn't. She sighed and looked again out the window. After a moment, she turned forward. "What about you? Do you have secrets?"

"Of course. Secrets are my line of work. That was true when I was in the Special Forces, and again now with Guardian Security. Keeping secrets is what I do."

"I'm not talking about other people's secrets. I'm talking about yours. Why are you so adamant about not mixing professional and personal?"

I swallowed, feeling my Adam's apple bob. The completely truthful answer was buried behind too many walls that I'd constructed over the years to even come close to revealing it. Instead, I told another truth. "I've already given you that answer, Dani. It blurs the lines."

"If we're personally connected, you can't protect me."

"No, it's that a personal connection" —I looked at her in the mirror— "...supersedes my knowledge and training. I swear I won't allow that, but I could act or react as the other person in your life, not merely as a bodyguard."

She tilted her head. "That seems better from my view."

"Better is a subjective assessment. Emotions are variables that are better left out of the equation."

"Does that mean...?"

I pulled up to the Metro Diner drive-through. There was one car in front of us. "Chicken Caesar salad or cheeseburger and fries?"

She grinned. "I can't believe you remember what I like to eat."

"I told you. I remember a lot about you. Which one?"

"Salad, no nuts."

As I set our order on the seat to my side, I turned back to Dani. "You asked what it means about leaving emotions out of the equation."

Dani nodded.

"It means I leave—as I did before."

She inhaled.

"I'm not fucking leaving."

Dani pressed her lips together and nodded. "I want to believe you."

"You don't have to." I put the SUV in gear. "I'll prove it to you."

"Even with the emotions?"

It was the wrong fucking answer, but it was also the one I knew in the depth of my soul that was true. "Yes. We can't deny they're there."

"I'm sure you'll figure it out. You always do."

It wasn't true. Nor was it that easy.

"I will."

With an app on my phone, I entered the code to open the garage door for the villa I'd procured. Since these villas were often rented for longer stays, I booked it for the next month. It would provide any of the Sinclairs with a home base when visiting Marsha. Currently, the primary bedroom would be for Dani. I'd take the queen-sized bed in the second bedroom and use the third bedroom for my home office. According to a text message from Mitchell Gray, Guardian had the villa secured, and the technology I'd requested installed.

After parking the SUV, I went to Dani's door. "I heard from Guardian. The villa is safe. You can come on up."

"No sweep? You're just going to trust them?"

My lips quirked. "If you want me to do a sweep...?"

Trepidation and uncertainty showed in the furrowing of her forehead as she stood and gazed around the small ground-level garage. "No, I'd rather go inside with you."

I entered the code from the Guardian and the door unlocked. Dani carried the things from her father's safe as the two of us stepped into the entry. While the blinds hid the illumination from the street, the first floor was aglow with lights. A modern kitchen was off to the left, and to the right was a living room with sliding glass doors that led to a secure lanai. "There are three bedrooms upstairs."

Biting her lip, Dani peered toward the staircase. "This place is bigger than I expected."

"It's better than hotel rooms and easier to secure. It's also large enough for when your brother and sister-in-law want to come down with their son."

Her eyes opened wide. "You didn't only rent it for two nights?"

"No. Continually finding new secure locations is a logistical nightmare. This villa will give us a home base close to your mother."

"For how long?"

"Currently a month."

Dani's cheeks rose. "That was thoughtful. Or is it just part of the job?"

I shrugged. "Maybe both. You want to be here for Marsha. I want you protected as much as possible. Jack and I spoke. This seemed like a good compromise. There's also the added benefit that there's a garage to keep the SUV less visible and more secure."

"Thank you, Eli." She looked around. "Where are our things?"

"They're still out in the vehicle. I'll bring them in."

"The food too."

A grin came to my lips. "The food too."

As I started walking toward the garage, Dani

called, "Eli?" When I turned, she asked, "Are there cameras, like Guardian put in Mom and Dad's villa?"

"There shouldn't be. I can double check."

She came closer and lowered her voice. "Audible bugs?"

I shook my head.

Lowering the bag to the tile floor, she reached her arms over my shoulders. "Double check. I don't want to get you in trouble for breaking the rules."

She was so fucking close.

I leaned my nose behind her ear and whispered. "Fuck the rules."

Dani took a step away, her pouty lips pursed together. "Make sure we're not being watched. Then we can discuss more about fucking."

CHAPTER

THIRTEEN

Dani

The way Eli's green gaze shimmered reminded me that there was life beyond my current prison, stuck within the bubble of despair and fear. That shimmer was a flicker of light in a dark world, and I intended to hold on with both hands.

"I'm glad you're here," I offered honestly. "I was upset when I first saw you at the cemetery, but..." I wasn't certain how to end that sentence.

"But...?"

"I feel safe with you." I looked around the first floor. "I want to be involved in this investigation, not just protected, if there's any chance I can help find who killed my father..."

He came closer. "From the first time I met you, you

impressed me with your knowledge. The few days I spent with you at Sinclair in R&D, I was blown away." He gave me half a smile. "A lot of my assignments lean toward the self-absorbed. They don't spend their days working on ways to make the population healthier."

"Dad cared about the people. He wasn't only in the business for the money."

Eli reached for my face, his warm palm cupping my cheek. "I didn't really know your father. I'm sorry about that."

The realization of my smile caught me off guard. "I can smile while thinking about him." I shrugged. "In ten minutes, I could be crying."

"That's the way grief works."

I stood straight, wondering if Eli knew that from experience.

Who had he lost?

"I know virtually nothing about you." I hadn't had the benefit of researching Elijah Rhodes before our first meeting. "Are your parents alive? Do you have siblings?" I looked down at his left hand and that ring. "Were you once married?"

"No, yes, and never."

I tried to recall the order of my questions. Before I could respond, Eli spoke. "That's more than I usually share. I don't want to lie to you, Dani. I never want to do that. However, there are questions I can't answer."

"Can't or won't?"

"Both."

I pressed my lips together and nodded. "I'm still

glad you're here. When it comes to your personal life, I can wait for you to share. When it comes to my father's case and your assignment—me—I want answers."

"Deal."

Kicking off my shoes, I lifted the beach bag from the floor. Eli gave me one last glance before disappearing through the door we'd entered back into the garage. Before I could decide if I wanted to learn the answers in this bag, he returned with both of our suitcases, my satchel, and the takeout bag.

As I watched him place the food on the kitchen counter, I asked, "Do you have any more gloves in that Mary Poppins pocket of yours?"

Reaching in his suit coat pocket, he handed me a pair. "Since it's not actually magical, I'll need to replenish my stock." He tilted his sharp chin toward the food. "Are you hungry?"

Tugging on my lip, I stared at the beach bag before meeting his gaze. "Should we eat first? What if something in this bag we find ruins our appetite?"

"I need to go upstairs and check out the computer setup Guardian made for me. You could eat now, or we could put the food in the refrigerator and settle in first."

Settling in sounded appealing.

"I want to go through Dad's things, but" —I shivered— "I'm nervous."

"I can do it."

I shook my head. "No. This is like what I just said. I

need to be involved. I'll take your support, but I must learn what he felt the need to protect."

"Will you wait for me?"

One quick nod and I tossed the gloves to the table. Looking down, I inspected the slacks and blouse I'd worn since we left Indianapolis. "I think I'd like to change. I'll check my emails, and then when you're ready, we can eat and then learn what secrets my dad had."

"Okay," he said, lifting the suitcases and heading toward the staircase. At the base of the stairs, he paused. "Are you headed up?"

I reached for my leather satchel, purse, and shoes and walked a few steps ahead of him. As it had been downstairs, every light was on as we entered the upstairs hallway. All the doors were opened, as if Guardian wanted to reassure us that everything was ready and safe. Outside the room with the large bed, I peeked inside.

"Do you want me to do a sweep?" Eli asked with a grin.

"No." I felt warmth gather in my cheeks. "However, that's not my way of barring you from the room."

He nodded. "Good to know."

I changed the subject. "I want to see the other rooms. What kind of high-tech setup did Guardian give you?"

After leaving my suitcase on my bed, Eli took his luggage to the bedroom across the hallway. I walked a step behind him as we entered the third bedroom.

My eyes opened wide. "Jeez, Guardian doesn't skimp."

"You can see now why we wanted a home base instead of hotel rooms."

The room no longer contained beds, dressers, bedside stands, or any furniture that would suggest it was a room where one was to sleep. The window was covered with a dark blanket over the blinds. Long desks lined three of the walls. Each desk contained at least two large monitors and multiple keyboards. There were two tall chairs on wheels and black boxes, I didn't recognize.

"What are those?"

"Scramblers." He shrugged as he removed his suit coat, revealing the holster strapped to his shoulder. "That's not their technical name, but it describes what they do. They make it more difficult for anyone to hack into our system or to have the ability to track our online movements."

I nodded. "EMI."

"In conjunction with interference technology. If," Eli continued, "the perp or even the police realize what we have going here, they could try to get access to our data."

"Like what happened with my parents' doorbell?"

"Yes and no." He removed his tie and opened his collar. "With your parents' doorbell, whoever took the boxes of journals stopped the doorbell from recognizing movement, thus stopping recording and notifications. In the case of anyone discovering our location, their goal would be to intercept our transmissions, searches, and data. We don't intend to share our information until we can prove who's guilty."

One of the screens caught my attention. I walked closer. "Is that the street camera from near the restaurant where Dad was shot?" It was as if a continuous slideshow of still pictures was playing.

Eli came closer and pointed to the corner of the screen where the time stamp continued to change. "Yes. We've gone back to three months before the shooting all the way to present. This program is searching for repeat license plates, makes of cars, anything that recurs."

"It's a popular location. I'm sure even Mom and Dad went there multiple times in that period of time."

"Once the program has the database of recurring items, it analyzes each one individually. Our working theory is that the shooter disappeared into someone's car during the chaos. Witnesses have been questioned and currently, no one claims to have seen him. However, given the time of day, there's no other reasonable explanation for his disappearance."

"That disputes your lone-wolf theory."

"Only if the person was planted and not also a victim."

My gaze went back to the screen. "Can you cross-reference the recurring cars or people with those people who have a connection to Sinclair Pharmaceuticals?"

Eli's green stare met mine. "We'd like to. Larry is

working with your brother for that information. We need that database." His eyes widened. "Can you get it?"

"Johnathon and Ella are working on that right now. My theory is that the shooter could be a disgruntled employee or consumer of Sinclair products."

Eli nodded. "We've had the same thought. The employee connection is easier to explore. Finding everyone who has ever taken a Sinclair -produced pharmaceutical is a huge undertaking." He pointed at the screen. "Often perpetrators do at least one dry run. There's a good chance that the shooter was at this location one or multiple times before encountering your father."

"He was carrying a sign, as if panhandling."

"Your mother can't recall exactly what the sign said. Jack didn't see it. And coincidentally, panhandling is illegal in the Villages," Eli said.

"I didn't know that."

"It's not illegal in the state of Florida, but it is within the community. Pretending to be a panhandler was a bold move. The shooter risked law enforcement intervention."

My forehead furrowed. "Then why do it?"

"Jack thinks it was to hide his weapon."

I pointed to Eli's holster. "There are other ways to hide a weapon."

"It's a working theory."

"Could the police have the sign?" I wasn't sure why I hadn't started asking these questions earlier. I could have asked the same things of Melinda. If I were to analyze the conundrum, I'd say I was in too much shock and buried in grief to look at the shooting from an objective point of view.

"No, they don't. It's disappeared with the suspect." Eli looked down at his watch. "It's getting late. You wanted to change clothes?"

"How long will you need to work up here?"

"Most of the night."

I sighed. "Okay. Do you have time to meet me downstairs in ten minutes for dinner and going through Dad's stuff?"

He pressed his firm lips together and nodded.

Back in my room, I quickly pulled a few things from my suitcase and made my way to the attached bathroom. While I hadn't planned to shower, the large glass enclosure was too inviting. I stripped out of my clothes and stepped under the warm spray. By the time ten minutes had passed, I combed out my wet hair and donned a pair of soft shorts and a tank top. I covered the tank with an oversized soft sweatshirt when I noticed the way my nipples tented the tank from the air conditioning.

That was definitely the cause—the cold air. My hardened nipples had nothing to do with the man down the hallway who I'd basically admitted to wanting to fuck.

Right.

I wasn't thinking about that at all.

My laptop remained in my satchel. My emails

would need to wait. I'd at least called Damien and left a message that Eli and I were settled in a villa. I told him it was nice, and he and Ella could use it later in the month.

As I made my way down the steps, I found Eli in the kitchen. He was still wearing his suit pants and button-up shirt. The only change was the way his sleeves were now rolled to his elbows, showing artistic tattoos on his muscular forearms, and the absence of his holster. His gun was lying on the kitchen counter. I looked around. "Where's the beach bag?"

FOURTEEN

Eli

The beach bag.

"I moved it to the living room," I said as I removed our dinner from the refrigerator.

Dani's posture relaxed as she came closer. Her wet long hair cascaded over her slender shoulders, and her beautiful face was free of the cosmetics she truly didn't need. Shapely long legs came from beneath an oversized sweatshirt. Her feet were bare, showing her light-pink toenails.

"Is the air too cool?" I asked.

"No." She wrapped her arms around her midsection. "I like soft, warm things."

"I did a sweep upstairs and down. There are no

cameras and no audio recording or transmitting devices."

Her lips curled as her navy-blue eyes met mine. "That's good to know."

"I also received a few text messages. Brian, Jack's nighttime replacement, is with your mother. She's resting peacefully."

Dani sighed as she sat at the kitchen table near where I'd set her salad and a bottle of water. Thankfully, Guardian had the refrigerator stocked with water.

"The other text was from Larry. All is quiet in Indianapolis."

She didn't respond. Her smile from upstairs was gone.

Handing her silverware, I tilted my head. "Are you having second thoughts about the things from your father's safe?"

She shook her head as she opened the lid to her salad. "I started wondering in the shower if it was fair for me to look through the things without Damien." Her blue eyes looked up. "He has as much right to know as I do." Before I could say anything, she added, "He isn't responsible for what happened, so don't go there."

I lifted my hand before taking the seat to her side with my dinner. "Do you think Darius is—capable?"

Dani prodded the lettuce around with her fork. "I don't." She looked up. "He and Damien have never gotten along." She pierced a chunk of chicken. "If I look at the whole situation from Darius's perspective, I get it. He was Dad's first child—first son. Then his parents divorced, and Dad married Mom. Darius was ten years old when along came Damien. Darius probably felt like he went from being the heir apparent to being left behind."

"Was he left behind?"

"No," she replied between bites. "When we were young, Darius spent every other weekend with us. Later, Dad gave Darius the chance to run Sinclair Pharmaceuticals, and he failed. It was so bad that Dad almost sold Sinclair."

I stopped arranging my sandwich. "Sold it? When?"

Dani hummed. "Well, Damien passed his five years of probation around a year ago. It would have been before Dad retired. I'd say maybe six years ago."

This wasn't in my research. "Was an official offer made? Who wanted to buy it?"

"I don't think there was an official offer. Dad was in informal discussions with people from Lilly, an Indianapolis-based pharmaceutical company."

"I didn't see anything about that in my research about Sinclair Pharmaceuticals," I admitted.

"Again, I don't think it got that far. Damien brought in Dr. Carpenter. The research and development of Propanolol was underway from a local university. Sinclair secured the rights and from that point, the development was fast-tracked." She smiled a glowing smile. "The rest is Sinclair history."

"So your father was going to sell the company and then changed his mind?"

"Damien changed his mind with Propanolol. In the early days of Sinclair, we mostly manufactured sterile saline, what's used in hospitals. Then in the 1980s after the Hatch-Waxman Amendments that allowed competition in drug prices, Dad went full throttle into generic insulin. Too bad we weren't making the GLP-1 formulas."

"The ones used for weight loss?"

Dani nodded. "They are now, but that wasn't their original objective. The GLP-1 drugs aren't new. They've been around for a long time for the treatment of diabetes. They stimulate the body's insulin, slow down the gastric process, reducing blood-sugar spikes, and decrease the secretion of glucagon, a hormone that raises blood sugar."

"They're all the rage." I was increasingly interested. Those drugs were on every other commercial or pop-up. "Did the GLP-1s hurt Sinclair's business?"

She shook her head. "They don't replace insulin if that's what you're asking. If Dad would have sold Sinclair to Eli Lilly, they would have had both the GLP-1s and have a corner on generic insulin."

"Doesn't Lilly make insulin?"

"They were the original manufacturer." She laid down her fork and reached for the water bottle, unscrewing the cap. "You don't think this has anything to do with what happened to Dad, do you?"

I leaned back against the chair. "I don't know. Was

Damien's introduction of Propanolol the reason your father didn't sell?"

"Basically. Dad was afraid Darius would run the family business into the ground. Being a footnote on a larger company was better than going bankrupt. After the promising results with Dr. Carpenter's research, Dad made a gamble to keep Sinclair Pharmaceuticals going."

"And Darius?" I asked.

"Damien replaced him. Darius has never forgiven him. He tried to get the position back; that's why you were hired a year ago."

I remembered.

"But things have changed. Darius has recently gone into business with Dwain Welsh from Moon Medical. They're making a mint as snake-oil sales-men." She shook her head. "Darius had no reason to hurt Dad."

"Snake oil?"

Dani scoffed. "That's what Damien calls it. They're capitalizing on the health-supplement market. That market has fewer regulations. It's easier to put prod-ucts out when you have a disclaimer saying that results are not guaranteed and to consult your physi-cian before use."

Dani's history lesson ran through my thoughts as I finished my sandwich. "Does that Dr. Carpenter still work for Sinclair?"

"No. He left right after Propanolol was approved for use."

Her answer caused me to bristle. "Why wouldn't he stick around to bask in the success?"

Dani sighed as she leaned back. "David...David Carpenter, was great. Even before I finished my PhD, he welcomed me into the lab and shared results with me. I thought it was just him being nice to the owner's daughter, but I think he truly wanted me to be a real part of the creation. He knew I'd be around after him."

"What happened?"

"After he retired from Sinclair—with a hearty retirement fund—he died."

My eyes opened wide. "Died? How? How old was he?"

"He wasn't old, close to fifty, I believe. His family kept the specifics of his death close to their vests. I suspect David was ill and just didn't let on. Once his research was finalized, he gave himself permission to move forward." She shook her head. "He lived and breathed Propanolol."

I made a mental note to find out what I could about Dr. David Carpenter.

Dani stood and gathered our empty papers and containers, depositing them into a trash can. "I'm ready."

A very distinctive part of me wanted her to be ready to do what she'd said earlier and discuss other fucking options. However, I knew that wasn't what she meant.

"Okay, I'll bring the bag back in here. The kitchen

table will be the best place to get a good look at what we found."

In the living room, I picked up the blue and white striped bag and carried it back to the kitchen. Dani's expression was blank as I came closer, as if she was unsure how she should feel at this moment.

"What will I tell Damien?"

I placed the bag on a chair between us. "I suppose that depends on what we find."

Squaring her shoulders, Dani nodded and donned the pair of latex gloves. I did the same, having retrieved another pair when I was upstairs. I removed my phone from my pants pocket. "I'm going to take pictures of everything for our team at Guardian. Sometimes they see things that can be missed in the moment."

Dani nodded and reached into the bag.

Some of the smaller items were the first to come out. She opened a velvet-covered square box. The diamond and emerald necklace inside was probably valued at over a hundred grand.

When she looked up, there were tears in her eyes. "This belonged to my father's mother. She left it to Mom, but Mom only wore it once. At Grandma's funeral."

"Didn't your mom like it?"

"There's more to it." She inhaled. "In a nutshell, Dad didn't have a sister, and the story was that originally, the necklace was to go to Sharlene." When I didn't respond, she added, "Darius's mother. According to Damien—I'm not sure how he knew—Sharlene asked for it in the divorce."

"Had your grandmother passed?"

"No," she said, aghast. "But she wanted it written in the divorce decree that upon Grandma Sinclair's death, the necklace went to her."

"Did you ever meet Sharlene Sinclair?"

"Oh yes." Dani wrinkled her nose. "She wasn't the nicest person."

"Today?"

Dani shrugged. "She went MIA about eight to ten years ago. Weird thing. No one knows where she is, nor have they heard from her."

"Even Darius?"

"He doesn't comment about her much. I remember Dad offered to pay a private investigator to find her. Darius said if she didn't want to be part of his life, good riddance." Dani lowered her voice. "The rumor was that she met someone—someone wealthy, no doubt—and didn't want to share her newfound bounty with her son."

Dani reached for a stack of small journals all tied together with twine. "These are what Dad had in the desk drawer. There were literally hundreds of them." She pulled on the twine. "Why would anyone steal them?" She opened the one on top.

The aged binding no longer held the pages in place. Carefully, she laid it open on the table. "1968."

Her bright blue eyes stared at me. "Dad was born in 1953. This was probably Grandpa Sinclair's journal."

"What does it say?"

FIFTEEN

Eli

Dani stepped back as I took a picture of the first page. The cursive writing was faded by time. There were few words. Mostly the text consisted of lines of letters and numbers.

"Those are chemical compounds," I said.

Dani leaned closer. "Formulas." She winked. "Basically, the same thing."

"When it comes to science, I bow to your superior knowledge."

Dani grinned. "When it comes to almost everything else, you win."

It was my turn to wink. "I was hoping you were going to tell me you'd bow."

Her cheeks filled with pink. "Back to the issue at

hand." She began to read the first one aloud. "C257H383N65077S6." Her blue eyes met mine. "That's Sinclair's formula for insulin."

"Did Sinclair have any involvement with its invention?"

"No," she answered quickly. "It was discovered by three Canadian scientists. In 1923, they sold their patent to the University of Toronto for only a Canadian dollar apiece. Lilly was granted exclusive rights to manufacture and distribute." Dani flipped through the pages. "It will take a while to read through all of these, especially if they're formulas. They're not all familiar. I'll need to research the chemical composition." She shook her head. "I definitely don't know all of these."

"Your father was a scientist like you?"

She laughed. "Dad was a businessman. Grandpa Sinclair was a scientist. My great-grandfather who founded Sinclair Pharmaceuticals did so by opportunity. Dad used to say the science gene skipped a generation."

"Why would Derek keep all these formulas if he didn't understand them?"

"Maybe because they were Grandpa's?" She closed the journal and stacked it with the others. "I'll take these up to my room and read while you're working on those computers."

I had a few programs running as we spoke. According to the Villages community website, pickleball was played every Monday and Wednesday morning at eight a.m. They probably wanted to get it done before the Florida sun scorched the courts. Pickleball lasted an hour, and the location of the courts was close enough to the Sinclairs' home for Carol to either walk or ride her bike. Even if she drove her golf cart, it was still a short trip.

Based on that primary data, Carol returned to her home after nine in the morning to find people coming to and going from the Sinclairs' home. Interestingly, there was no activity on the Sinclairs' camera doorbell.

It didn't take me long to learn the doorbell companies representing the neighbors. My current search was working to find the necessary codes to hack into each of the closest neighbor's database. The incident was recent enough that assuming not all the doorbells were scrambled, we should have more information.

I reached for the photo album. "Do you want to look through this?"

Dani exhaled and nodded again, wrapping her arms around her midsection.

"Are you all right?"

"Cold."

I picked up the photo album and reached for her hand. After a puzzled look, she stood as I led her into the living room. "Here." I motioned toward the couch, and she sat. I sat beside her, laying the closed album on her lap.

When Dani shivered, I laid my arm around her shoulders.

Dani stiffened.

"I wanted to help you warm up." I started to move my arm. "But I don't—"

She snuggled against my side. "I don't want you to move your arm." Her navy-blue stare peered upward. "I'm just unsure of where we are in this rule-breaking journey."

"Fuck if I know."

That made her grin.

"This is new territory for me too." Running my thumb over her cheek, I gently pinched her chin, lifting it until I was again staring into her gaze. "Since your comment about fucking, it's taken every ounce of my self-control to not throw you over my shoulder like some caveman and carry you upstairs." I scoffed. "I've also imagined bending you over that kitchen table."

"Yet, somehow you've refrained."

I tipped my chin toward the album. "If we have answers here, we need to find them."

Dani reached for the album and moved it to the coffee table. "I want answers."

"You need them to get your life back."

She shimmied closer. "I know you have work to do." Her eyes were back on mine. "I'm tired of navigating all of this alone."

Pulling her closer still, I kissed her pert nose. "You're not alone any longer."

Her eyes hooded.

"Talk to me."

Dani shook her head. "The practical part of me, the

part that manages all aspects of my life, has a million questions. I'm not alone—but for how long? What will happen when we find the killer?"

I started to speak, but she laid her finger on my lips.

"I don't want answers, Eli. I want to step away, even for a short time, from my crushing solitude. I don't want to think. I want to feel."

Solitude.

Alone was how I'd lived most of my life. I knew exactly what she was talking about. There was that sensation that even amongst a crowd, I was truly by myself. That was the world I'd created for myself, and I did it well. It was why my bank accounts runneth over. It was why Ben always had a new job waiting for me. I'd traveled the world and yet none of it was particularly memorable. It was simply my job.

The money and the sights were background noise.

I didn't deserve to have more than that, but here she was—the gorgeous woman who had been living in my head for the last year. She was real and within my reach.

"Come here," I said, my timbre slowing.

When Dani looked puzzled, I reached for her waist and lifted her over my lap. After squirming, she wrapped her sexy legs around my waist. My cock grew with the knowledge her pussy was hovering inches away, separated only by our clothing.

Holding Dani's waist in place, I met her gaze. "Tell

me to stop, because if you don't, I'm going to begin to do all the things I've thought of doing to you."

"You've thought about me?"

Reaching for the hem of her sweatshirt, I pulled it over her nearly dry hair and found a light green tank top beneath. "Every fucking day since the first time I saw you in Damien's office." My lips curled. "You were wearing a white lab coat."

"Oh, so sexy."

"Made me hard."

"You're lying."

I shook my head. "I wouldn't lie to you, Dani. You're making me hard right now."

She wiggled her pussy against my growing erection. "I know you're telling the truth now."

"Last chance, tell me to stop."

"Don't stop."

Splaying my fingers beneath the fabric of her top, I caressed the soft skin above her waist. Dani arched her back, pushing her breasts against me. Our lips came together as they had earlier in the day. She fucking tasted like sunshine and clouds. My goal was to wipe away those clouds so she could shine her blinding glow.

My tongue teased the seam of her lips. Without hesitation, she allowed me entry. Our faces moved, our tongues danced, and the air filled with erotic sounds.

Again, I reached for the hem of her top, pulling it

over her head. A growl slipped from my lips at the sight of her heavy breasts, her deep-red areolas, and her tight nipples. A dip of my head and I seized one nipple between my lips. Dani squealed as I nipped the hard bud with my teeth. My assault moved from one breast to the other, over and over, until her fingers were woven through my hair and her breathing was erratic.

The idea of carrying her over my shoulder was appealing, but since I'd determined that the living room was free from monitoring, I did the next best thing, lifting her off my lap and placing her onto the couch. In one swift move, I snagged the waistband of her shorts and then her panties, pulling them both down past her ankles. The sweet scent of her essence filled my senses as I lowered my kisses—beyond her breasts, down over her stomach, over the swell between her hips.

"Eli."

My name echoed throughout the villa as I buried my face between her legs. She was so fucking wet as I lapped her sweet cum.

Her hips bucked as I teased her clit.

I wasn't sure when it happened, but my hair was no longer gathered at my neck, but hanging free as I lapped and teased.

Dani pulled away and reached for the buttons on my shirt. "I want a more even playing field."

The desperation and desire in her tone was as

erotic as the sweet taste of her pussy. I sat back as we both fumbled with the small buttons. She splayed her fingers over my chest. It was as I was about to remove the sleeves from my shoulders that the doorbell rang.

Dani's wide eyes met mine. "Who is it?"

CHAPTER

SIXTEEN

Dani

L ike the shattering of crystal, our bubble broke. The doorbell's ring reverberated throughout the villa as I tried to make sense of what was happening. My heartbeat raced as the symbolic crash littered the floor with glass shards. Undeterred by the possible danger, Eli stood, his massive body a barrier between me and the door. My scrambled thoughts came together.

Someone was outside.

Somebody wanted inside.

Goose bumps prickled my flesh at the newest revelation.

I was naked—completely nude.

Quickly, I searched for my clothes, finding my shorts and panties on the floor and my tank top hanging off the coffee table. As I scrambled to cover myself, Eli buttoned his shirt, tucking it into his pants.

"Go upstairs," he ordered in a hushed tone.

"I want..." I wasn't certain what I wanted.

"Fuck." His green stare searching the room. "My gun."

"It's in the kitchen," I replied as I pulled the sweatshirt over my head and reached for the photo album.

Eli went to the kitchen for his gun as the second ring of the doorbell ricocheted throughout the villa. "Dani, go upstairs now."

I grabbed the photo album and the stack of journals as I hurried up the steps. I knew from earlier that at the top of the landing, I'd be hidden from the first floor. Once I reached that area, I stopped, hugging the meager possessions to my chest as my pulse echoed in my ears. Straining, I tried to hear what was happening on the first floor.

"Mr. Rhodes," an unfamiliar male voice said.

"I'm Elijah Rhodes."

"I'm Special Agent Timmons, and this is Special Agent Wilson with the FBI. We have some questions for you."

"Do you have a badge?" Eli asked.

"Of course." Pause. "Sir, my partner and I would like to come inside."

"Do you have a warrant?"

"No, sir. We have a few questions. May we come inside?"

"Absolutely not. What is this about?"

My hands trembled as I bit my lower lip, and my cyclone of thoughts swirled out of control.

"The murder of Derek Sinclair."

I covered my lips to mute an audible gasp.

"Do you have new evidence?" Eli asked.

"We'd like to ask you and Dr. Sinclair some questions." There was a pause. "Is she available?"

"She's retired for the evening. If you have questions for us, we can meet you tomorrow at your field office."

"Our closest field office is in Jacksonville. We'd like to clear this up tonight."

Eli was unflappable. "Dr. Sinclair is unavailable. If you take a step back, I'll come outside, and you can ask me whatever questions you may have."

"I'm afraid, Mr. Rhodes, we call the shots here." The man's voice deepened. "Wake Dr. Sinclair. Agent Wilson and I will wait."

"Remain outside," Eli said.

"You have two minutes."

Two minutes.

What the hell is happening?

The front door closed. I could only assume Eli engaged the lock. His footsteps on the staircase were too few, as if he was taking them two or three at a time. Coming around the corner, he nearly plowed me over. "Fuck."

"What's happening?" There was something unusual in Eli's expression. Could it be fear? "Eli?"

"They're claiming they're FBI, but the badges are fake."

"Are you sure?"

He nodded, looking down at what I was holding. "They shouldn't fucking know we're here." He ran his long fingers through his hair and met my gaze. "Without a warrant, they can't come in the villa. But for safety's sake, hide those things in your suitcase or satchel."

I'd almost forgotten what I was holding. "Um, okay."

"We'll go down together and speak to them on the driveway. Where's your phone?"

"Plugged in in the bedroom, why?"

"Go get it."

I didn't hesitate to follow his instructions, placing the photo album and journals in my suitcase and covering them with clothes. Next, I went to where my phone was on the bedside stand and took it to Eli.

Once I handed the phone to him, Eli entered the passcode and opened the camera. "Take this to the window in your room, the one that looks down on the driveway. Place it in the window. I have cameras pointed outside, but since I didn't get a notification upon their arrival, I'm assuming they're scrambled."

"Fake FBI, scrambling signals." I looked up. "What's going on?"

His lips curled. "At the sight of your hair, they won't doubt you were sleeping."

I smoothed my hair with my hand, convinced that I looked a nearly fucked mess. I asked my question again. "What's happening?"

"I don't know. I think we should play along to try to figure out their game plan."

Play along. I could do that.

I nodded.

Peering around the plantation blinds, I saw a dark SUV parked in the driveway and two men in dark uniforms standing beside it. They were talking to one another, not looking up as I placed my phone in the window.

When I returned, Eli was donning his suit coat over his holster. As his eyes met mine, he said, "Only concealed carry is legal in Florida."

I took a deep breath as we both walked down the staircase. Eli opened the front door. The two men came toward us as we stepped outside. The sidewalk beneath my bare feet was still warm from the day's earlier sunshine, yet the air had chilled.

"Dr. Sinclair," the taller man said. "I'm Special Agent Timmons."

Crossing my arms over my breasts, I was thankful for the sweatshirt. "Special Agent, what is this about? Do you have a lead in my father's murder?"

"Ma'am, we have reason to believe someone illegally entered your parents' home this evening."

My gaze went to Eli and back to Special Agent Timmons. "What happened?"

"Two individuals were seen carrying a bag away from the house."

"Was the house entered illegally?" I asked. "Windows broken? Door pushed in?"

"No. However, it's come to our attention that like many of the residents in your parents' neighborhood, security codes are often shared."

I inhaled, hoping that honesty was still the best policy. "We were at my parents' home this evening. You see, my mother is in a nearby physical-rehab facility, and she asked for a few personal items."

"What did you take?" he asked.

Eli stepped forward. "Are you looking for something in particular?"

"Doctor," Special Agent Timmons said, "what did you remove from your parents' home?"

"Reading glasses, underwear, cosmetics...my mother had a list."

"Have you taken those things to Mrs. Sinclair?"

"Some of the things," Eli said. "Once we delivered them, Mrs. Sinclair realized she wanted a few things that weren't on her list. That's why we returned to the house. It was late. Our plan is to deliver the other items tomorrow."

"Did your mother request items from your father's safe?" Special Agent Timmons asked me.

His safe.

What the actual hell?

My gaze went back to Eli and then to the special agent. "I was in my parents' bedroom. I didn't see a safe."

"You're unaware of a safe in your father's office?"

I shrugged. "He mentioned that once, now that you bring it up."

"We have reason to believe that safe was accessed earlier this evening. Let me cut to the chase. We believe the two of you went illegally into the Sinclair house and stole the contents of the safe."

My neck straightened as I squared my shoulders. "I have POA for my mother. Entering her home is not illegal."

Eli stepped forward. "You don't have a warrant. We've answered your questions. Any further questions will need either a warrant or be conducted in Jacksonville."

"Sir, we could take you both in."

"You won't," Eli said definitively. "If you had evidence, we wouldn't be having this discussion right now."

"We have evidence." Agent Timmons showed a grainy picture on his phone of Eli and me leaving Mom's villa with the striped bag. "If you could bring us the bag."

Eli placed his hand in the small of my back. "Good night, Special Agents."

"Doctor?" the second agent asked.

"We're done," Eli said.

"Doctor, it would be in your family's best interest for us to see what you removed from the safe."

"My attorney will be in touch." That was my reply. With that, we turned back toward the villa.

Once inside, Eli shut the door and engaged the locks.

"What the hell?" I asked when his green stare met mine. "Was that a threat?"

CHAPTER

SEVENTEEN

Dani

Eli's jaw clenched as his nostrils flared. "A fucking obvious one." He lifted his hand. "I need to find out how they knew the safe was accessed and how they found us."

I shook my head and hurried toward the kitchen. The blue and white striped bag was on the chair where we'd left it. Eli was a step behind me.

"What do you think they want?" I asked, peering into the depths.

"Just a minute."

I stood puzzled as Eli hurried up the stairs. In less than a minute he was back with my phone in hand. "I want to ask Carol tomorrow if these uniforms" —he showed me the paused video on my screen— "are similar to the people who she saw last Wednesday."

Without gloves, I dumped the contents of the bag on the kitchen table, creating a momentary ruckus as I scanned the variety of items.

"Dani, you should be wearing gloves."

Inhaling sharply, I turned to Eli who was now behind me. "I have every right to go inside my mother's home. I don't understand what those men thought they were doing."

He reached for my shoulders. "Intimidation. That's what it was."

I peered upward into his green stare. Unlike earlier, his orbs were solid green, calm, and reassuring. "You were scared earlier, when you came upstairs for me." It wasn't as much a question as it was a statement.

"I was concerned," Eli admitted. "I knew they weren't real FBI, and I didn't know what they had planned or more importantly, how they found us."

"I've never seen you anything but stoic."

He ran his large palms over my shoulders and down the arms of my sweatshirt. "It's the fucking blurred line. You mean more to me than an assignment."

"I was scared for you, too."

He leaned closer and kissed my hair. "Don't worry about me. If anyone would have not made it through that meeting, it would have been them. I just don't reach for my gun as the first option. I wanted to hear what they had to say." His smile grew. "They thought you would be an easy mark to intimidate, and they were wrong. If you have that attorney you mentioned on speed dial, I suggest you let him or her know that something is off."

"Seriously?" I spun, looking for a clock. "It's after nine o'clock."

Eli nodded. "The more people who know the better." His gaze met mine. "Have you spoken to anyone since we got here?"

"No. I left Damien a message."

"Do the two of you share your location on your phones?"

"Yes, but..." Shaking my head, I thought about my attorney.

I hadn't spoken to Stephen since the cemetery. If he'd sent me information on Preston Ayers, I hadn't had the chance to look at it. "Fine, I'll call him." My gaze went to the table covered in things. "What about all that?"

Eli reached in his suit coat and pulled out another pair of gloves.

I quirked a brow.

"I told you I restocked." He tilted his chin toward the stairs. "I'll put this all back in the bag and take it up to your room. I have a few theories, and there may be answers upstairs in the computer room. You can either go through these things in there or in your room."

I looked around the first floor, remembering our unwelcome visitors. "In there with you. I don't feel like being alone."

Despite my desire for togetherness, I spent nearly the next twenty minutes in my bedroom in conversation with Stephen Elliott, the head of Sinclair's legal department, and a close friend of my father's. When he mentioned Mr. Ayers, I told him the truth. I hadn't checked my emails. I told Stephen about the visit from the FBI or fake FBI.

He advised me that Eli's answers were correct. No law enforcement officer may legally enter a house or even a rented villa without a warrant. That warrant must specify what the law enforcement officers were searching for. Rarely was a blanket search warrant issued. However, if during their legal search, they came across illegal material or substances, those too could be confiscated. "I don't have anything illegal." My gaze went to the striped bag.

Did Dad have something illegal?

Stephen laughed. "Dani, I've known you all your life. I highly doubt you would have anything illegal. I'll contact the Jacksonville field office tomorrow morning and check on the identities of Special Agents Timmons and Wilson."

"Thank you," I replied as I pulled the large manila envelope from the bag with my gloved hands. Turning it over multiple times, I spoke, "Can I ask you something?"

"You can ask."

That felt like Eli's answer when he said there were times he might not be able to give me the answers I wanted.

"You knew Dad well."

"My best friend."

"Did Dad have any secrets that could have led to his death or something he was hiding?" I pried the metal clasp open.

I couldn't open the envelope without tearing the paper.

Stephen replied, "I've been thinking about that since the shooting. I can't think of anything. Derek was a shrewd businessman, but he wasn't unethical and wouldn't do anything illegal. He was fair with his employees and with the business. You said you opened his safe. Was there anything there?"

"We haven't gone through all of it yet. Did you know Dad had hundreds of my grandfather's and great-grandfather's journals?"

Steam. I could steam it open. I tried to stay focused and listened to Stephen.

"Oh yes. Derek could spend hours reading those over and over."

"The ones in his desk drawer are gone."

"Gone? They were there when I was there."

My forehead furrowed. "You looked in Dad's desk?"

"Yes. It's where I found his insurance papers and will."

"But you had a copy of his last will and testament at your office."

"Right, but I was afraid if he hadn't destroyed the old one, there would be consequences. Remember, the clause about selling Sinclair? He rewrote the will after his illness."

That was right.

"Why do you think Dad liked those journals so much?" I asked.

"I don't have a good answer for you. I can just say that he derived pleasure from knowing the family business was still going strong, despite ups and downs."

"Were there downs that were more severe than I realized?"

"Dani, we should talk in person. You could ask Damien."

"When?" I pressured.

Stephen sighed. "During the dark Darius days was probably the worst that I can remember. I was tasked with investigating if Chapter 11 was the right route for Sinclair."

I gasped. "I thought Dad was thinking of selling to Eli Lilly."

"There were multiple options. Lilly's offer wasn't what we expected. Thankfully, Sinclair secured the patent on Propanolol and all that was avoided."

That was a lot for me to think about. "Thank you, Stephen, for taking my call so late."

His tone lightened. "Give my love to Marsha, and when you're back home, we can chat."

"Goodbye." My stomach twisted as I disconnected the call.

Carrying the envelope, I walked from my bedroom to the computer room. For a moment, I stood in the door frame, watching as Eli worked. His intense gaze was glued to the screen, his forehead furrowed with concentration, and his untethered hair curled to his sharp chin. He was so enthralled as his long fingers flew over the keyboards, working between three different stations at the same time, I almost hated to disturb him.

Finally, I said, "Hey."

His piercing green stare met mine. "Hey." His gaze swept over me from my messy hair to my pink toenails. "You're fucking stunning."

Warmth filled my cheeks. "You said I had bedhead."

Eli scoffed. "I said they'd believe you were in bed. That doesn't mean you aren't beautiful." He smirked. "It's hard for me to look at you and not think about my face buried between your legs."

Thankfully, the sweatshirt would hide my hardening nipples. "That all ended rather abruptly."

He nodded. "It did." His gaze landed on the envelope. "What did you find?"

"I don't know." I lifted it. "Tearing it open seems wrong. I was thinking about steam."

"That would work."

As Eli stood, he seemed to double in height. The sight of his shirt reminded me that we had unbuttoned it earlier, and I ran my palm over his muscular chest.

He pointed to the door. "Let's take it in the small bathroom in the hallway. We can turn on the shower and let it run for a while."

My lips curled. "That's a good idea."

As we entered the bathroom, Eli turned on the shower, setting the dial to hot. I placed the envelope precariously on the top of the glass door. The flap hung over the spray, close enough for steam, but not to get wet.

"That should do it," Eli said. Stepping back into the hallway, he asked, "How was Mr. Elliott?"

I shrugged as we walked together back to the computer room. "He was glad I called. I told him what happened. Tomorrow he's going to call the Jacksonville FBI field office and check on the two agents." I took a few steps closer, running my fingertips over the sleek desk. "He and my dad were friends and colleagues for my entire life—longer. Stephen even traveled down here with Damien and I after the shooting. I asked him if Dad had any secrets."

Eli sat in the chair he'd just vacated and leaned back. "And...?"

"He said no, nothing earth-shattering."

I peeled the latex gloves from my fingers and placed them on one of the desks.

Eli's gaze went back to the screen before him. "Do you want to see what I've found?"

Excitement sounded in my tone. "You found something?" It was the first ray of sunlight in this dark nightmare. I moved closer, standing at his side and peering at the screen.

CHAPTER

EIGHTEEN

Dani

Eli used the mouse to point. "This is an aerial schematic of your mother's neighborhood. This is her home. This one is Carol's. Most of the houses in the Villages use Ring security cameras. A recent string in the neighborhood app had multiple complaints about their security being down." He pointed the mouse on the screen. "But see this house, the one across the street from your parents'?"

"Yeah. I'm not sure who lives there."

"I have the name of the owner. That's not important. According to an application they filed with the homeowner's association, the owner rents the house out six months a year. I can only assume, that because it's rented, the owner wanted a more dependable security."

"Not Ring," I said.

"Ring isn't bad, but what this house has is high end, as good as Guardian's." He looked at me with a sexy grin and winked. "It is Guardian's."

That bubble of hope grew larger in my chest. "That's good, right?"

"It's very good. The frequency that was used to scramble the Ring monitors didn't disable the Guardian one."

"Can Guardian's security cameras not be disabled?"

"They can," he said. "You must know what you're dealing with. I contacted Ben and he was able to get the footage I needed. Let me show you..."

Eli spun his chair toward another keyboard and his long fingers flew, click after click. "Look."

I followed him to the next screen. The vision before me was a long-distance view of the front of Mom's house. The black SUV in the driveway could be any SUV. "I see a license plate."

"Very good. Ben is running that now. Here...watch the people coming and going."

I did. Their uniforms were exactly like the two men who visited us tonight, and as Carol said, dark but not marked with a department. The uniforms of the sheriff's deputies who had stopped by were clearly marked as county. "They're the same people."

"The same group. It's hard to get facial recognition, but I'm still trying."

"What do these people want with Dad's journals?"

Eli leaned back and reached out, tugging my hands until I came right to the side of his chair. "This is something. It's not the answer, but it's *an* answer."

I crossed my arms over my breasts and leaned against the desk. "If they knew Dad had a safe, why didn't they access it then?"

"Another good question."

"Thank you." I bent down, lowering my lips to his. The connection warmed my circulation in the opposite way the doorbell had earlier caused my blood to cool.

Eli's hands roamed under both of my shirts. "Where were we?"

I shook my head. "The mood is..."

"Gone?"

"For now."

He scooted back his chair and tugged me forward until I was sitting across his lap. With his stunning stare only a few millimeters away, he teased rogue stray hairs away from my face. "Sex can wait. But having you close with my rules out the window..." He kissed my nose. "I fucking love touching you whenever I want."

I laid my hand over his wide chest, feeling the strong rhythmic beat of his heart. "As long as that goes both ways."

Reaching for my hand, Eli kissed my palm. "I could

get used to that." He tilted his head as he stared into my eyes. "Is there something else bothering you?"

"You mean, besides my dad and whoever those men were?"

"That's what I mean."

I laid my cheek against his hard shoulder and inhaled, soaking in his warmth and inhaling the remnants of his cologne. Eli wrapped his arm around me, holding me to him with his strong embrace. I tried to recall my recent phone conversation. "Stephen said something I didn't know." I looked up, meeting Eli's gaze. "He said that during the dark Darius days, he'd been tasked with investigating Chapter 11."

"Business was that bad?"

I shrugged. "I didn't realize. Maybe Damien is right to hate Darius."

"What happened?"

"I'm sure Damien could tell us more. From what I was told, Darius knew we needed more than generic insulin and saline to keep us viable, but Darius was terrible at management. He had multiple different formulas in development." I shook my head. "He wanted to get Sinclair into anti-anxiety and antidepressant medications."

Eli furrowed his brow. "Did you say earlier that Darius is now working with Dwain Welsh?"

"Yes, on natural wellness products."

"But...I'm trying to recall from when I worked with you before. Correct me if I'm wrong, but Moon

Medical, Welsh's company, specialized in anti-anxiety medications."

I sat straighter. "You're right."

"Do you think they were working together back then?"

"That doesn't make sense." I pressed my lips together. "Why would Darius want in on Welsh's market if they were friends?"

Eli shook his head. "Darius wanted to diversify…"

"Right, but he was spending too much money on too many things. Development is expensive. That's why when Damien found Dr. Carpenter and the research on Propanolol, a never-before marketed formula, he convinced Dad to turn off Darius's pet projects and concentrate on just one."

Quickly, I turned toward Eli. "You said your camera outside was disabled?"

"I haven't looked at it, but it didn't send a notification that those two phony agents were at the door."

My pulse sped faster. "Your camera is Guardian."

Eli agreed.

"If it was scrambled, the men that were here knew it would be a Guardian camera."

His eyebrows knitted together. "They had to. They also knew we opened your dad's safe."

"How?"

"That's what I'm trying to figure out."

The blue gloves reminded me of the envelope. "Do you think we can open the envelope now?"

"I'd rather keep you here on my lap. My cock likes the feel of your tight ass."

Grinning, I wiggled my behind.

Eli growled. "You're killing me."

I lifted my palm to cup his cheek, feeling his scruffy beard growth. "There's been enough killing. I want you to keep living and keep breaking your rules."

Slipping the gloves back on, we went to the bathroom. The air within was thick with warm steam. My first look at the shower stall caused me to gasp. The envelope was gone. Looking down, I saw that it had fallen to the floor. "Thank goodness it didn't fall in the shower." As I squatted down to pick it up, I saw that the flap was open.

Eli turned off the shower.

Standing with it in my grasp, I met Eli's green stare. "What did Dad think needed to be protected?"

Tilting his head, he led me back to the computer room and cleared a space on one of the desks. My hands trembled as I pulled the single page from within. My pulse quickened at the sight of my father's handwriting.

Eli stood by my side as we both read.

IF THIS IS EVER FOUND, *my worst nightmare came true. I pray it was only me that he came after and that those I love are safe.*

The decision wasn't easy, but given the circumstances, I

would do it again. No price is too high to save that which was built.

Don't question.

Don't let the truth come out. I'll take it to my grave; let it rest there. Please, to those who know, keep your word, for the sake of my family and legacy.

Derek

A TEAR SLIPPED DOWN my cheek as I turned to Eli. "What does this mean?"

Tendons in his neck bulged as his jaw clenched. "It's cryptic to say the least."

"Dad had a fear of someone retaliating against him. Who and why?" I reread the note. "No price is too high...did he pay for something or someone?"

I laid the paper on the desk and removed the gloves.

Eli's deep voice broke through the cyclone of racing thoughts within my mind. "Your father was murdered. It wasn't random. It was because of a decision he made." He reached for my chilled hand. "Do you have any idea?"

"No."

Eli wrapped his arms around me like a warm blanket as I laid my head against his shirt, the beat of his heart and the sound of his voice caused his wide chest to vibrate. "Fuck, Dani, this was what I didn't want. I don't want you to change your opinion. We don't know exactly what Derek did."

My temples ached.

"I'm too in shock to know what I think."

A single tear.

It was all I shed.

Eli's large hand rubbed soft circles on my back.

The man I admired most in the world brought on his own death. What would Mom say? What about Damien and Ella? Dylan? My heart ached. Dylan would never remember his grandfather and now, what would he be told about the once-great man?

I looked up. "Can we please take a break? I don't want to learn anything else at the moment."

Eli nodded and kissed the top of my head. "Are you ready for bed?"

"Only if I'm not alone."

Dani

Not a word was spoken as I held tightly to Eli's hand, leading him away from the earth-shattering revelation we'd uncovered to the bedroom that was ordained mine. The lamp near the bed glowed, casting a warm golden circle on the ceiling above and a slightly larger one on the nightstand below.

Dropping his hand, I turned, facing the same buttons I'd worked to undo earlier in the evening. The urgency of that encounter was gone, replaced by something softer and deeper. Eli's green orbs again swirled with golden flecks, a kaleidoscope of desire as I meticulously released each button. It was when Eli removed his shirt that I finally got a good look at the ink scrolled on his chest. Slowly, I walked around the man who had been the star of my fantasies for the last year.

No longer in my imagination, Elijah Rhodes was flesh and blood. My fingertips trailed over his muscles, examining each hard plane and every indented valley. I stepped around him, admiring the firmness of his abs and shoulders. The dark ink swirled as I read. "De oppresso liber?"

"From oppression, we liberate them," Eli translated. "Special Forces."

Keeping my hand on his arm, I looked up. "I can't imagine all the atrocities you've seen in your life."

"I'd never want to share those memories." His hands came to my waist. "I did what I had to do. It's why as a bodyguard, killing isn't my goal. I want to keep you safe without taking another life. However, know that if I had to, I would."

I swallowed. "You had to in the Special Forces?"

He nodded. "I've heard others say they don't remember how many. I do. I wish I didn't."

Eli didn't share the number, but that was all right. I could hear the remorse in his deep timbre. This mostly stoic man was capable of taking lives, yet that wasn't his calling; saving and defending was why he put his own life on the line.

I couldn't think about the person who purposely shot my father—he'd obviously wanted to take a life.

Lifting my hands to Eli's broad shoulders, I pushed up on my tiptoes. "Let's not remember. Not remember *anything* right now. I want to live in the present. Just you and me."

His lips came down on mine, possessive and assured. I let myself get lost in his touch as my sweatshirt, tank top, shorts, and panties made their way to the floor. With each ensuing second, sparks came to life beneath my skin. The world was lost as Eli unbuckled his belt, the clasp clattering on the floor, the swoosh of his zipper seconds before his pants fell to his ankles. After kicking off his shoes, Eli took a step away, leaving a black puddle of expensive suit pants.

Almost nude, Eli's muscular body was only covered by black silk boxer briefs. The bulge beneath was growing larger by the second.

"My turn," he said as his penetrating stare scanned my naked body. He walked a complete circle around me as I had done, his warm touch tantalizing my skin. His focused stare was like a laser heating me from the inside out. Butterfly kisses tickled my shoulders and breasts. "You're sensational, Dani."

Framing my face, his lips came back to mine. Step by step, he moved the two of us until I was trapped between two unmovable objects, him and the wall. Eli reached for my ass and without effort lifted me until my arms were around his shoulders and my legs around his waist. He didn't hesitate to find my folds with his long, skilled fingers.

I moaned and stretched my neck back, my head against the wall as he plunged one and then two fingers deep inside me. My body hummed like a well-tuned guitar, and Eli was the musician, the aficionado who knew exactly what strings to strum and what melody to play.

Within his grasp, my body bounced to his tempo. His scruffy cheeks abraded the soft skin on my neck and collarbone in the best of ways. It was as his thumb circled my clit that I called out. Whatever I said wasn't articulate. I wasn't even certain it made sense. I was completely absorbed in the dueling sensations.

As the temperature reached a fevered pitch, Eli pushed down his boxers, freeing his cock. My body stiffened at the initial invasion. Despite our foreplay that had me wet and ready, I sucked in a breath. His girth and length were more than I'd ever experienced. My fingernails carved crescent moons in his shoulders as we each worked to accommodate the other. Once he was fully buried, I laid my forehead on his shoulder and exhaled. A slight wiggle of my hips and the vise grip my core had on him loosened enough to turn discomfort into pleasure.

Pleasure.

It was a word I'd never fully comprehended until that moment. The fullness was overwhelming and rewarding.

Eli's intense green gaze met mine. "I've dreamt about this."

My cheeks rose as a smile bloomed. "About me—*us*?"

He nodded. "The last year, I tried, but I couldn't get you out of my mind."

"You too. I mean, I never forgot you." I wiggled my hips. "I never imagined that being with you would feel this good."

"Doctor, we're just getting started."

The mattress jiggled as Eli lowered me to the bed, our connection never fully severed. My body tingled from my head to my toes as Eli pushed my knees back. His stare zeroed in as he pushed in and pulled out. "My cock is fucking shiny with your cum."

I imagined what he described.

Our rhythm was off until it wasn't.

Together, we moved in sync, two separate people finally finding their way together. My first orgasm built from a spark to a flame and into a roaring inferno. The damage would be devastating if not for the unrelenting attention to detail coming from the man above me, the man tending the fire with care.

Eli didn't stop as I spiraled down. It was as I was once again earthbound that he unexpectedly pulled out, the loss left my core clenching at the sudden emptiness. He flipped me to my stomach and tugged my ass upward until I was on my knees. I sucked in a breath as without hesitation, he buried himself to the hilt, regaining our connection. If the first round was his gentler version, the second round was a race to the finish.

I didn't feel the orgasm coming. There wasn't a warning sign or flashing light. It struck from out of the darkness, a freight train barreling down the tracks in a darkened tunnel. Words and whimpers came from my lips as my body convulsed, and fireworks exploded behind my closed eyes.

Three more thrusts and Eli stilled, the room filling with his roar as he shuddered inside me. My knees gave out as his weight held me to the mattress. I could stay as we were for the rest of the night.

Safe.

Warm.

Cared for in the cocoon of his body.

Alas, that wasn't to be.

Memories flooded my mind.

The letter.

The hint of something I didn't think I wanted to know.

Yet for an undetermined amount of time, Eli had done as I asked. He'd taken the world away and given me a reprieve.

TWENTY

Eli

I stayed with Dani until she drifted to sleep. My body wanted to stay at her side, but that letter had my thoughts spiraling. There was a secret to learn. Since the fake FBI agents were involved, I could only assume they were the ones who didn't want the secret to get out, or quite possibly, they were paid by someone to let the secret die with Derek Sinclair.

Dani had a long day with her mother tomorrow and sleep would be best. I, on the other hand, functioned without the recommended eight hours. On most nights, during an assignment, I was lucky to get four hours.

Dani's questions also had me wondering.

How did the fake agents know I'd have Guardian

Security equipment? It wasn't like we drove around in panel vans with the company logo on the side. How did they know where we were staying? How did they find us here?

The obvious possibility was an improbability. The other souls from Guardian Security; there was the owner, Ben, the lead on this assignment, Larry, Jack Webb, and Brian, his night- shift replacement. There was Melinda—though she wouldn't know where we were currently staying. And then there was Ella's guard in Indianapolis, Deidra Burton. I'd worked with Deidra on many assignments over the years. I couldn't let myself believe that any of those individuals would compromise an assignment. Not one person on that list spiked my suspicions.

My thoughts searched for possibilities outside of Guardian Security. There were people from the hospital and physical-rehab facility that were privy to the name of our company—again they wouldn't know where we were staying. We'd told the two county deputies earlier in the day that I worked for Guardian Security.

Could the county sheriff's department be in cahoots with the fake agents?

As more questions emerged, I recalled Dani's stories about Sinclair Pharmaceuticals, the dark Darius days, and Propanolol. The scientist who made it all happen.

I ran a search on Dr. David Carpenter.

His name wasn't unique. There were numerous

physicians with the same name throughout the country. There was an OB-GYN in Washington State. But the David Carpenter Dani mentioned wouldn't be alive. Dani said he'd passed away. My next search was for David Carpenter, obituary, Indianapolis, Indiana.

Bingo.

The information was short—too short.

DAVID J. *Carpenter passed away in Avon, Indiana, at the age of 51. He was born in Carmel, Indiana, to Donald and Carol Carpenter. He married Brenda Marie Olsen Carpenter. Together they had three children: Eric Carpenter, Julie (Michael Sawell), and Louisa (Grant Hills). David's journey included achieving Lieutenant in the US Navy, PhD in molecular fusion, and a fellowship at Indianapolis University Research. David was survived by his mother, wife, children, and four grandchildren. Donations can be made to the Foundation for Medical Research.*

WHY WOULDN'T they mention his prestigious work for Sinclair Pharmaceuticals?

By two in the morning, I left the computers running with more searches as I went to the bedroom across the hallway from Dani's room. In the hallway, I paused and looked inside her room, remembering every second of what we'd done a few hours earlier.

While Dani was currently asleep, she must have woken up at some point. No longer was she as I'd left her, fully nude. Curled up under a sheet, I saw she was wearing her tank top and panties. The lamp near the bed, the one that I'd turned off, was again shining. Lying next to her in the bed was the open photo album from her father's safe. Moving the album to the bedside stand, I turned off her light. For a moment I hesitated, wanting to bend down and leave a kiss on Dani's cheek.

My reason for not doing that was complicated.

For the first time in years, I not only wanted to protect a woman, but I desired more. Having Dani in my arms was invigorating. Touching and caressing her opened a part of my soul that I'd kept closed and buried since the day I'd put my heart on lockdown. What happened earlier tonight fractured that hard dark cover I'd secured around my heart. Dani had blown that casing to smithereens.

There was debris to tend to if I were to move forward.

Back in my bedroom, I opened my satchel and took out my personal laptop. It was something I always carried with me, yet I never used it for work purposes. As I brought the computer to life, a battle raged within me.

I needed to do this.

I owed it to both of them.

Using my fingerprint, I opened the computer. The file wasn't difficult to find, even though I hadn't accessed it in ages. Another code was needed to open the folder. My heart clenched in my chest as Amy's face filled the screen. The photograph was a casual shot, a picture I'd taken only days before her death. Her curly blond hair blew in the breeze, and her lips were upturned in a smile. We'd been hiking at a state park in Oregon. Little did we realize during that moment that soon we'd be called for the same job.

Amy wasn't my assignment; she was my coworker, a fellow Guardian Securities bodyguard. It was a line that never should have been blurred. Like myself, Amy had prior military experience. Her skills on a shooting range exceeded—hell, anyone else's. My assignment was a client in witness protection. He'd turned state's evidence against a powerful man with underworld connections. The client was scheduled to testify in a federal trial on the second day of our assignments.

I was assigned to the man testifying. Amy was assigned his wife.

The transfer to the courthouse was supposed to be routine. The plan was to take two cars to the court-house. I knew Amy was capable. We both completed our routine pre-inspection of the cars, discussed the best routes.

A normal day.

At the last minute, we decided to switch vehicles as an extra safety measure. My assignment and I made it to the courthouse. Amy and her assignment didn't.

An incendiary device had been placed into the gas tank in the car I should have been driving. Even my complete inspection of the vehicle failed to find it. On their way to the courthouse, the device was activated.

"I miss you," I whispered, or spoke in my mind. I wasn't sure. Reaching out, I touched the screen. "I meant everything I said to you. I saw a future for us. I wanted that. You were stolen away, and I swore I could never love again." I inhaled. "I think I was wrong. There's something about Dani." My cheeks rose. "I think you'd like her. She's strong like you. You'd kick her ass on a firing range, but she'd kick yours in a research lab. I guess I just wanted to tell you that for the first time since you left me, I want to smile. I want to protect her and keep her safe. I guess I'm talking to you, to defend my right to love. That doesn't mean I'll ever forget you. I won't. I've been given another chance, and I promise you and Dani, I won't make the same mistake. I won't let my love for her blur the lines in a way that could risk her life."

For a moment, I stared at Amy's picture, knowing it would be the last time I saw it. "I hope you can rest peacefully, knowing I'm trying to live, trying for more than work, and also trying to remember what love is. I owe you that."

I kissed the tips of my fingers and touched the screen. My chest ached as I deleted the folder. As difficult as it was to say the final goodbye, it wasn't fair to Dani for me to hold on to my past.

Dani and I had talked about grieving. I knew the process well.

As I shut down the laptop, I took off the gold band from my left hand. I hadn't lied to Dani. I'd never married. That ring worked for the reason I told people.

It also reminded me that at one time I'd wanted to marry.

I still did, but if it happened, that commitment deserved a new ring.

I made myself a promise. If Dr. Danielle Sinclair would have me in her life after this assignment was complete, I'd stay.

Because as much as I tried to walk away from her a year ago, the pull to return was too strong. I'd find who killed her father and was terrorizing her family, and after that, I'd devote myself not only to her safety but to her happiness.

One more sweep of the doors and windows, and I stripped to my boxer shorts and slipped under the covers. If I had my way, it would be one of the last nights I slept alone.

CHAPTER

TWENTY-ONE

Dani

When I woke up, instead of grief, for the first time in weeks, my thoughts were positive—memories of Eli. In hindsight, the two of us moved pretty fast from *why are you back* to *full steam ahead*. And yet, as I stared up at the ceiling, I didn't regret a minute. The feelings I'd harbored for him over the last year came out with a vengeance. It could be said that our physical attraction was my way of distracting myself from the tragedies of life. However, as I recalled the way in which we came together as one, I wanted to believe there was more.

Does he feel the same?

Last night, sometime after Eli slipped away, I woke. Unable to fall back to sleep, I decided to start looking through Dad's photo album. The photographs were in no particular order, some dating back to when Dad was in high school and later, college at Purdue University. Others were more recent. It was the older photographs that had me stumped. I could identify family, but there were others taken in the offices and labs at Sinclair that contained people I didn't recognize.

I tried not to read too much into the fact that Eli left my bed and my room. He had work to do. Those thoughts took me back to my dad's letter. After taking care of business, I decided I wanted to read Dad's letter again.

Down the hallway, I found Eli working behind one of the computer screens. Instead of his usual suit, he was ruggedly handsome with his facial beard growth, his hair untethered, wearing basketball shorts and a Colts t-shirt. My heart may have fluttered a bit. "Good morning."

He looked up, his handsome green stare scanning from my head to my toes. His cheeks rose as his lips curled into a devilish grin. "Good morning."

I walked closer. "I've never seen you look so casual."

Eli scooted his chair back and reached for my hand. "You, Dr. Sinclair, are witnessing the breaking of many rules."

"I would think Elijah Rhodes was a by-the-book kind of man."

"He has been." Eli tugged me down to his lap and brought his lips to mine. "Until you."

I palmed his scruffy cheeks. "This rogue side of you is extremely sexy."

"All of you is sexy."

"For the record," I said, "I don't usually sleep with someone the second day."

Eli's smile grew as he caressed my cheek. "Dani, last night wasn't the second day; it was a year in the making. The moment I saw you at the cemetery, I wanted to wrap my arms around you. Last night was the best sex I've had in a long time." He sighed. "I want you more than I should." He lowered his tone. "I could take you back down the hall right now."

Warmth filled my cheeks.

"But..." he said, letting the word hang in the air a bit. "When I woke up this morning I had some thoughts about your dad."

Dad had been my second thought. Ignoring the sudden chill, I looked around the room at the items on the desks. "Where's his letter? I wanted to read it again."

Eli exhaled. "I sealed it and had it couriered to Ben at the main Guardian office in Philadelphia."

My forehead furrowed. "Why would you do that and when?"

"About six this morning. They'll run forensics. I

want to know if there are any fingerprints on the paper other than your dad's. They'll also do a handwriting analysis to be sure it's his writing. If we're lucky, testing can determine the age of the paper and ink. If we know when it was written, it would be a clue as to what he mentioned—his decision."

"It was Dad's writing. I'd know it anywhere."

"We should have more answers by tomorrow."

I sat taller. "What other concerns did you come up with this morning?"

"We've gotten the attention of the wrong people. I believe that someone suspected there was damning evidence in Derek's possession that would lead to their involvement. I ran facial recognition on our two special agents." He shook his head. "We didn't have a great view from your phone, but I did get a hit on the one who called himself Timmons."

"Called himself? As in, that's not his name. What did you find?"

"Last night, after I pulled myself away from your warm bed," Eli said, "I received confirmation that the Jacksonville FBI has two agents by the name of Timmons and Wilson."

What?

I blinked as my lips opened. "I'm confused. I thought you said they were fake badges."

"They were. I was able to pull up photographs of the two real agents. Their resemblance to the real agents isn't even close."

"Interesting, they used real names..." I let that

thought stew for a moment. "Did you let the FBI know that there are people impersonating them?"

"I didn't," he said. "I don't want to let on to anyone that we know. I need to find out more about the two impostors. I believe they're our connection to Derek's killer."

A cold chill covered my arms with goose bumps. "Do you think they killed him?"

"I think they're somehow involved."

"What about your lone-wolf theory?"

He shook his head. "With your dad's letter, I believe there's more to this."

"We should at least tell the sheriff's department what we've learned." I clutched my hand in my lap. "Aren't they supposed to be investigating this?"

His head bobbed. "Why do you think they are?"

"I'm sorry, what? You don't think they are? They came to the house yesterday when we were there."

"Yet they didn't interfere when the people were removing things from your father's office. What I don't understand is why the thieves didn't open the safe if they knew of its existence. Those safes aren't that difficult to crack."

"They must not have known about it."

He nodded again. "My conclusion too. How then did they find out that we'd opened it?"

I inhaled and exhaled. My fingers went to my temples. "It's all a big jigsaw puzzle, and I don't think we have all the pieces."

"At this point, I'd be happy to have the outline in place."

I stood, pacing near his chair. "A disgruntled employee would have gone after Damien, not Dad." I spoke my thoughts aloud. "A patient upset with their medication would have gone after Damien. This wasn't random. Whatever decision Dad made is why he's dead."

"Agent Timmons is actually Chad Broadrick." Eli scooted his chair to the desk, hit a few keys on the keyboard, and brought up a picture of the man whom we'd spoken to last night. "He's had a few run-ins with the law and even done some prison time. Basically, he's a gun-for-hire."

My eyes opened wide. "So you do think he killed Dad."

"I don't know. I think that there's a good chance that someone else is pulling the strings. More than likely, the shooter was hired. He wasn't alone. To disappear the way he did, he had help."

"Cue his sidekick, Special Agent Wilson."

Eli shrugged.

"What did Dad do, the decision he referenced, to warrant killing him?"

"I'm more concerned about why and how they found us here. If they're afraid you found evidence, you're in greater danger than before."

I closed my eyes and sighed.

"Dani, keeping you safe is my top priority. I think we should head back to Indianapolis today."

"I told Mom I'd be here until Sunday." I looked at my watch. It was nearly eight. "I need to be to the facility by ten. She's supposed to meet with the physical-therapy team. I want to be in on their plan and learn how long she'll be in rehab. I also want to ask her about some of the people in Dad's pictures."

"While you're there, Jack can watch over you. I'm going to try to pull some strings and get us back to Indy today." He met my stare. "Call your brother to send down the plane."

"If I call Damien, he's going to ask why I'm coming home early and honestly, I'm not sure what to tell him. Maybe we're wrong about Dad. I don't want to be the one to tell Damien if we don't have all the answers."

I hated to leave Mom a day early, but at Eli's prompting, I packed all my things, including the items from Dad's safe. He secured them all in the back of the SUV.

As Eli drove me to the physical-rehabilitation facility, my mind was overwhelmed by what we'd learned and all the questions we still had. On the seat to my side was the striped beach bag containing only one item, the photo album.

From the back seat, I could see Eli's wide shoulders and the top of his head. The rugged handsomeness from earlier this morning was gone; his immaculate bodyguard persona was back in place. Eli's hair was again tethered at the nape of his neck. His muscles, the ones I felt flex against me last night, were covered by his tailored dark suit and white shirt.

Eli's sunglass-covered gaze went to the rearview mirror. "How are you doing?"

"Confused and scared." I watched the scenes pass by the SUV windows. "Maybe going back to Indy today is best." I sat taller. "I'm not going to tell Mom about the letter. I don't want to put her in more danger."

He nodded. "I think that's best."

TWENTY-TWO

Eli

I parked the SUV behind the facility and walked Dani to the employees' door. At only nine thirty in the morning, the temperature was already oppressive. Why anyone would want to live in Florida's relentless heat was beyond me. The cool air conditioning met us as we stepped inside. Thankfully, there were no employees wandering the back hallways. My hand made its way to the small of Dani's back. The urge to keep her close was overpowering.

Up one flight of stairs, we found ourselves close to Marsha Sinclair's room. Jack was at his post, sitting outside her room. He stood as we approached. A few inches shorter than I, Jack Webb was still a formidable man. His shaved head gave him a look of distinction and made it difficult to estimate his age.

"How is Mom today?" Dani asked Jack.

"She's tired and sore. I think all the tests and exercises they ran yesterday were too much."

Dani tipped her head toward the closed door. "Is she alone?"

"Yes."

Dani's navy stare met mine. In the depths of the blue, I saw what she'd said in the vehicle. I saw the fear that I wanted to erase and the uncertainty I vowed to quell. She nodded before opening the door and slipping inside.

I turned to Jack. "How long have you been working the Sinclairs?"

"Ben put me on the job about six months ago. I replaced Leo Conner."

I'd met Leo a few times. "Why did he leave?"

Jack shrugged. "I didn't ask."

Pressing my lips together, I nodded. "In those six months, you never examined the contents of Mr. Sinclair's safe?"

"No. He said it was private. I respected his wishes."

"Did you mention the safe to anyone yesterday after we spoke?"

"No. Did you find anything?"

I shrugged, not comfortable with full disclosure. "A few of the old journals. Jewelry. His coin collection."

Jack furrowed his brow. "Wait a minute. I did. I spoke with Mr. Sinclair yesterday. The subject of the safe came up. Yeah, now I remember. I thought it was odd after just talking to you about it."

"Mr. *Damien* Sinclair?"

Jack nodded. "He was checking on Mrs. Sinclair. I told him that his sister was going to check the safe. He mentioned that he didn't think anything of importance was there. Seems that he and the attorney, Elliott, searched it, looking for Derek's insurance papers."

"When?"

"Right after the shooting. Mr. Elliott came down with Damien and Danielle. Elliott was real broken up. Damien said Mr. Elliott was Derek's oldest and dearest friend."

"There weren't any insurance papers inside the safe. Did Elliott and Sinclair find what they were looking for?"

"I'd assume as much. He didn't say."

"Dr. Sinclair," I said, "wants to be with her mother for the meeting with the physical-therapy unit. Will you keep an eye on her? I have a few things to get wrapped up before we need to get back."

"I thought you were staying until tomorrow."

"That was the plan. Will you watch Dani?"

"She'll be safe. No one is getting past me."

"Good to know," I said.

Back in the SUV, I called Benjamin.

"Good morning, Eli. Just the man I was about to call. How is your assignment?"

My assignment.

Dr. Danielle Sinclair.

Dani.

"Safe for now," I replied. "Some things have me concerned. I also wanted to find out what you learned about the virus I found on her electronics."

"Jackie just brought me that report. That's why I was about to call."

Jackie was Ben's assistant.

"What did you find?"

"The virus is called GONO78, the same one Jack found on the Sinclairs' computer and phones and was found on Damien and Ella Sinclair's electronics. Are you familiar?"

"No."

"In a nutshell, it continually searches for keywords. It's hard to say if this virus was placed by someone looking for information about Sinclair's business or personal. It's not extremely high tech and can be sent easily through an email or text message."

"Do you know how long it was there?"

"Not yet. We do know that it wasn't there a year ago when you first worked the assignment."

"Can you see the location of the receiver?"

"Not yet," he replied. "We're working on tearing through some firewalls. At this point, we know the virus was transmitting to the greater Indianapolis area."

"Fuck," I growled.

"What else is concerning you?" he asked.

I proceeded to tell him about the events of last

night. "I can't figure out two things. One, how did those guns-for-hire find us? The SUV was in the garage. I booked the villa under an LLC. Second, how did they know we'd gotten into Derek's safe?"

"What's your gut telling you?"

"Jack Webb said he spoke to Damien Sinclair yesterday. He mentioned something about Dani wanting to get inside the safe." I inhaled. "What do we know about Damien Sinclair?"

"He's the man who hired us."

"And his father was killed under our watch."

"I ran a conclusive background check on him before taking him on as a client last year."

"Did you run his financials?"

"Of course."

"Run them again," I said.

"Eli, this is highly unusual."

"Run both Damien's and Darius's. For the record, they're both in the greater Indianapolis area. I want to know if either of them has a significant amount of outgoing funds in the past two months."

"You think that Derek Sinclair's killer was paid."

"It's what my gut is telling me, Ben. I sent a picture of the safe to the main office to ask about the number of digits the combination would require. I spoke to Jack. Dani spoke to her mom. Unless someone from Guardian is in on this, the only other people who knew we wanted in that safe were Marsha Sinclair and Damien Sinclair. I don't believe Marsha would arrange to have herself shot." Although stranger things have happened.

"I'll run a report."

"Ben, there's a package coming to you today. I had it sent through a courier. I need the forensics on the letter ASAP."

"You do know we have multiple assignments in progress."

"You told me to listen to my gut. I'm listening. I need you to do what you can do. Those men came to the villa that was supposed to be safe. They found Dr. Sinclair. I don't like that. The other thing I need is a plane this evening to Indianapolis."

"Commercial?"

"Charter. Use a different LLC."

"I'll have Jackie work on this for you. She'll get you set up."

Another person who would know our plans.

"Thank you, Ben. I'm about to meet up with Mitchell Gray. He's getting me some surveillance equipment. Tell Jackie to check with him. Dr. Sinclair and I are flying under false identities. Only Guardian will know. I sure as hell hope that there isn't a mole in this company."

"There isn't. I'd bet my life on that."

I wasn't betting Dani's life.

"I need to go."

TWENTY-THREE

Dani

"It sounds like you'll be busy," I said to Mom as I helped her back into bed. "With all that therapy, in no time, you'll be having dinners in the dining room instead of in here."

Mom looked down at the tray of food and back to me. "What if it isn't safe?" Her lip quivered. "I've been alone since Derek died. I don't know if I can trust other people."

"Mom." I sat on the edge of the bed and covered her hand with mine. "Maybe along with the physical therapy, you need to talk to someone, a counselor or therapist. You've been through a very traumatic series of events."

"I just want to close my eyes and wake up next to

your father. I want to be annoyed by his snoring. I want to find his chair at the kitchen table pulled out because he rarely thought of pushing it back into place. I want to find his coffee cup in the sink because the dishwasher was too much to ask." Tears streamed down her cheeks. "I'm sorry, Dani. I shouldn't burden you with this."

"You're not burdening me, Mom. I love you. As soon as you're able, you're coming to Indy. You don't have to sell your place or make any rash decisions, but you are alone too much. I'm sorry I can't stay longer."

"I understand." She reached for a tissue and wiped her eyes and nose. "I know I can't have all the things I just listed, but I hope one day we can all have peace. They need to find whoever did this to your father."

Pressing my lips together, I nodded. "They will. Guardian Security is working on that as we speak."

"And the police and FBI."

"Of course." I sat taller. "Have they come to talk to you?"

"Back in the hospital. Deputies from Sumter County came multiple times."

"You mentioned FBI."

"They only visited once. Two men." She looked around. "The sheriff sent female deputies." She smiled. "They were kind."

"Did you get their names?"

"The deputies? I think they gave me their card. I don't remember."

"The FBI."

Mom shook her head.

"What did the FBI ask?"

Mom picked up her fork and began pushing the green beans, mashed potatoes, and meatloaf around her plate. "The same questions as the sheriff's deputies. What could I remember? Had your dad told me anything that I believe would have endangered him. Had he been acting oddly." She took a bite of meatloaf.

"Had he been?"

"Acting odd? No."

"Did Dad ever say anything that you think could be connected?"

Mom shook her head. "There is no logical reason why anyone would harm Derek. He was a good husband, father, and person." Her expression fell. "He was so excited to be a grandfather."

I feigned a smile. "We'll all tell Dylan great stories about his beloved papa." I noticed the blue and white striped beach bag. "Mom, I found a photo album, and I was wondering if you could help me identify some of the people."

"Sure, bring it here."

I took the photo album and laid it on the covers next to her. "Finish eating first."

She reached down and opened the cover. A smile curled her lips. "Oh my. Look how handsome your father was." She shook her head. "That was before I knew him."

I came around and peered down. "How old do you think he was?"

"I'd say around twenty. He was in college." She took a drink of her water. "And look" —she pointed to the man at Dad's side— "that's Phen."

Leaning down, I took a closer look. "Phen?"

"Oh, he doesn't go by Phen any longer, but Derek always called him that. Stephen Elliott. He and your father were roommates their freshman year and in the same fraternity."

I picked up the album and stared at the faded picture. "Goodness, I didn't recognize Stephen. I knew this one was Dad."

After Mom finished eating, I moved her tray and placed the album on the rolling table. Slowly, she went through, page by page. Naming every face. There were pictures of Darius as a baby. Damien and I at different ages. There was a picture of Dad standing in front of Sinclair Pharmaceuticals and one of him in front of the scrolled word Sinclair outside the executive offices with a big smile. It was right after a big remodel.

"This one," I said, pointing. "I recognize the research area at Sinclair, but I don't know who this person is."

Mom tugged the photo from the plastic sleeve and turned it over. On the back was written *Eric*. Pressing her lips together, she hummed. "I believe that was Eric Olsen."

"A chemist at Sinclair?"

"No, no. He was a research fellow at Indianapolis University."

"Was? Is he dead?"

"Oh yes, it was years ago. Tragic really. He was shot in broad daylight."

A cold chill skittered down my spine. "Like Dad."

"I guess." Her eyes widened. "That's a coincidence. Eric was at a park, sitting on a bench. It was sad." She met my gaze. "You remember David Carpenter?"

"Yes."

"His wife, Brenda, was Eric Olsen's daughter."

"What was Eric's research focus?"

She inhaled. "I believe it had something to do with the Propanolol that David engineered. After Eric was killed, the university shut down its research. Damien convinced David to come to Sinclair and complete his father-in-law's research and development."

"Didn't David die unexpectedly?"

"He was ill. Derek knew, but David didn't want anyone else to know." She shrugged. "I haven't thought about Brenda in a while. I wonder how she's doing."

"Her father was killed and her husband died young. Poor Brenda."

"Well, financially she was secure."

"How do you know?"

"David turned Sinclair Pharmaceuticals around after Darius..." She pursed her lips. "Damien might know more of the particulars, but getting David to work for Sinclair was a feat. Of course, he was well compensated."

My phone buzzed. I read the text message from Eli.

"*WE HAVE A FLIGHT TO CATCH.*"

I TURNED TO MOM. "I'm sorry I'm leaving early. I'll fill Damien in on all your therapies. I'm sure Ella or Damien will be down here soon. I'll be back too."

She reached out for my hand. "Stay safe, Dani. I don't want anything to happen to anyone else I love."

Just like Dad's letter.

I feigned a smile. "I will, Mom. I have Eli."

"Last time he left."

"Because last time there wasn't really a threat."

"I hope he stays," she said. "Sinclair can afford Guardian Security, and until Derek's case is resolved, I feel better if he's with you."

My smile was genuine. "Me too."

I hoped he stayed.

I hoped the murderer would be found.

I hoped Eli would stay after that.

"Do you mind if I keep the photo album?" I asked.

"Oh, I'm enjoying these memories. I think I'd like to keep it for now. It will give me something to do."

How could I say no to that?

"Okay, Mom. If any picture jumps out at you, please let me know."

"It's nice to remember the happier times."

After giving her a kiss, I picked up the empty bag and opened the door. A stunning green stare met me from the other side of the hallway. Eli's arms were crossed over his chest, stretching his bodyguard uniform on the shoulders. His long legs were crossed at the ankles.

As he dropped his arms and pulled away from the wall, a grin tugged at his lips. "Dr. Sinclair."

"Mr. Rhodes."

I turned to Jack. "Thank you for watching over Mom. It would be okay if you went inside. I think she's lonely."

Jack nodded.

Eli lifted his hand in a wave before placing it on the small of my back as we made our way to the back stairs.

"Dr. Sinclair," a woman called from the nurses' station.

We stopped as the woman came closer. I didn't need to see her name badge to know who she was. "Becky."

"You were present during your mother's therapy-planning session."

"I was."

She handed me a clipboard. "It seems that somehow you entered without signing in downstairs. Please sign by the X. We make a point to keep our patients safe with up-to-date records."

As I signed, I had a thought. "Do you know if the

hospital Mom was transferred from has the same protocol?" I was trying to recall right after the incident, but honestly, it was all a blur.

"Yes."

"So," I asked, "if I wanted to check on some of Mom's visitors, they'd be able to tell me?"

"They should. Every visitor is supposed to sign in, give the name of the patient they're visiting, and sign out when they leave." She took the clipboard. "Are you now leaving?"

"I am."

She scribbled the time of day on the page before handing it to Eli. "Sir, could you also sign?"

He nodded as he wrote Elijah Rhodes, the date and time.

Becky didn't stop us as we made our way to the back steps. It wasn't until we were out and back inside the SUV that Eli asked a question as he pulled the vehicle away from the curb.

"Who do you want to check on, what visitor to your mother?"

"Mom said two FBI agents visited her at the hospital. She said the Sumter County Sheriff's deputies came multiple times. The FBI only once."

"What does she remember about the FBI?"

"Just two men. Couldn't recall their names."

"Are you wondering if they were real?"

I lifted my brow. "I am. Wouldn't Jack check their credentials? He'd know they were fake, right?"

Eli inhaled. "I don't know what to think. I'll ask him if he recalls the visit."

"What about the whole work setup in the villa—all those computers."

"I spoke to my contact this afternoon. Guardian will clean it out. The location is compromised." He handed me a small wallet. "For the flight back, you will be Candace Rogers. I'm your husband, Lloyd."

"Lloyd," I said with a giggle. "You could pick any name, and you chose Lloyd?"

"Mitchell already had the IDs. I didn't get a choice."

"Why are we not us?"

"Because at this exact time, I don't trust anyone." Through his sunglasses, he looked into the rearview mirror. "Have you called your brother to tell him you're coming home early?"

I reached for my purse. "I should."

"Don't."

TWENTY-FOUR

Eli

The Citation CJ2 was sleek, the inside small enough that I had to duck or hit my head. With six passenger seats, Dani—a.k.a. Candace—and I had more than enough room. The pilot introduced himself as Leonardo Alexander. The copilot was Kara Crawford. Jackie had opted out of a flight attendant. Considering the flight time was barely two hours, we would survive. Nevertheless, I stopped on the way to the airport and picked up chicken salad sandwiches for our dining pleasure.

"Mr. and Mrs. Rogers, there is coffee, water, and a selection of beers and wines available," Kara said. "I could get you something now, or you're welcome to help yourself once we reach cruising altitude.

"Thank you, I'm fine for now," Dani said as she took a seat with her back to the cockpit. I tapped her shoulder and motioned farther toward the aft, away from the cockpit. Once she was again seated, I sat across from her, facing the cockpit. Between us, a small table extended from the wall.

When Dani removed her laptop, I shook my head. "Why?"

My cheeks rose as I tried for my most charming smile. "Because I want to talk to my wife as we fly over the clouds."

Dani quirked an eyebrow. "I haven't checked my emails in two days. Do you have any idea how many there probably are?"

I watched the flight crew as they made their way down their checklist, suspicious that they could hear whatever we said. Lifting my hand, I laid it on the table, palm up.

Dani looked wary, yet she finally placed her hand in mine. "What's happening?" she asked in a whisper.

"I'm currently trying to keep you safe. Sadly, I'm questioning everyone and everything." I lowered my voice. "I don't trust the internet on this plane." I shook my head. "No emails until we're to your home."

"Is that why you didn't want me to call Damien?"

I pressed my lips together as my nostrils flared. "It's more than that."

"Stop it. My brother isn't capable of having anything to do with hurting our parents."

"You're sure?"

Dani nodded. "One hundred percent." She looked down at my hand, the one holding hers. "Where's your ring?"

I scoffed. "My timing to remove it wasn't good."

She wiggled her fingers on her left hand. "It's okay. I forgot mine too."

Kara appeared at our side. "Mr. and Mrs. Rogers, if the two of you are ready, we will take off soon." She smiled. "Please be sure your seat belts are fastened."

Once she walked away, Dani scanned the interior of the plane. "This is extravagant. It's probably more expensive than calling for the Sinclair plane."

"Your brother can afford it. Unless he's short on cash."

Dani's blue gaze met mine. "Why would Damien be short on cash?"

"There're rumors of a recession. I'm not privy to how that relates to the pharmaceutical industry."

"Our products are necessary. Our saline production had to double last fall. The only other plant in the country that makes saline is in North Carolina. Their production was stalled due to the hurricanes. They're back up now, but we were having a terrible time keeping up."

"I didn't know that."

"Damien hired you, Larry, Deidra...I'd venture to say his cash flow is fine."

"Larry let me know that he has set up a new computer network in your second bedroom."

Dani's eyes opened wide. "As big as you had in that villa?"

"Not quite. I need a bed."

Her eyebrows danced. "We might be able to arrange something."

I swallowed. "Not a fact I want Larry to report to Ben."

"I was talking about the couch."

I chuckled. "Of course you were."

"Is Larry picking us up?" Dani asked.

"Yes. Currently, other than Jackie at the main office, Larry's the only one aware of our arrival."

"And you can trust him?"

"I have." I moved my suit coat, showing Dani the holster. "Private planes don't require TSA screenings. I'll inform Mitchell I still have it when I contact him."

"What did you do today while I was with Mom?"

With the sound of the engines, and the headphones over our pilots' ears, I felt more comfortable talking, to a degree. "I went to your mother's house and set up some new hidden cameras."

"Who do you expect to see?"

"I hope our FBI guys." I went on, "The virus I found on your electronics is a searching tool. It's set to find keywords in your communications, text messages, emails, and even documents."

Her eyebrows knitted together. "What keywords?"

"We haven't determined that."

"But the virus is now gone, right?"

"Yes."

"You said Mom and Dad's computer had it too?"

I nodded. "Damien's and Ella's also."

"Did you find out anything else?"

"They're still working on pinpointing the server. All Guardian could tell me was that the information was being streamed back to the greater Indianapolis area."

"No." Dani shook her head. "It's not Damien."

"There are roughly two million people in the greater Indianapolis area. Why would your thoughts go to your brother?"

"Because of what you've said." She pressed her lips together.

After a moment of watching clouds, Dani turned back to me and told me about showing the photo album to her mother. The old memories made Marsha happy, so Dani left the photo album with her.

"Did your mom remark on why Derek would have saved those particular photographs?"

She shook her head. "There was one of Dad and Stephen Elliott in college. I'd forgotten that they were roommates their freshman year."

"Why didn't Stephen retire when your dad did if they're the same age?"

"I don't know. I think he wanted to stay with Sinclair and help Damien succeed."

"Did you know he and Damien went through your father's safe right after the incident?" I asked.

"No." She sat straighter. "Who told you that?"

"Jack."

"Last night when I spoke to Stephen," Dani began, "he said he looked in Dad's desk." She pursed her lips. "I didn't give it much thought at the time, but he said the desk was where he found Dad's will and insurance papers. But Mom said Dad didn't keep important things in his desk, but rather in his safe."

"Maybe Stephen meant the safe."

"Maybe. I'll ask Damien."

I remembered our sandwiches that I'd put in the small refrigerator. "It's late for lunch or early for dinner. Do you want your chicken salad?"

Dani unclasped her seat belt and met my gaze. "Shoot, I forgot to tell you, I can't eat nuts."

"I'm a step ahead. I read your bio the first time I was assigned to you. I made sure there were no nuts in the chicken salad."

Her cheeks rose. "All about protecting me." She winked. "I'll get the sandwiches and a water. What do you want to drink?"

"Water is good. I don't drink alcohol on the job."

Her smile curled. "Now that you mention it, I've never seen you with alcohol."

"You like wine."

"I do."

"Once we have you completely safe, we'll celebrate with a bottle of the best wine I can buy."

"Sounds like a date."

It was barely five o'clock when we landed in Indianapolis. As I took my phone out of airplane mode, it buzzed with missed messages. I hit the icon for voice-mail. Ben's name appeared.

"Eli, we have the preliminary forensics on the letter you sent. Call me as soon as you have time to talk."

TWENTY-FIVE

Dani

Back in my condominium, I sat in my office at my desktop computer, going through the hundreds of emails I'd managed to avoid until now. Preston Ayers's CV was among the masses. Eli was in his new office, formally my guest room. He was right; the setup wasn't as big as the one in the villa. Yet, he assured me that he had much of the same capability. If there was anything he couldn't do with the new setup, he could ask the people in Philadelphia to do it for him.

The sky beyond the windows was dark, the lights of downtown twinkling below. On a Saturday night, the sidewalks were bustling with people. While football season was in full swing, the large venue was constantly booked with other forms of entertainment. Basketball was just beginning. The city was a beehive of activity.

Leaning back against my chair and staring out the window, my thoughts went to my mother. She said she'd been alone since Dad's death. I understood that feeling. If it weren't for Eli down the hallway, I would feel alone.

Honestly, while I wasn't alone, without the ease and freedom of those walking the sidewalks, I had the sensation of being trapped. I also feared that I'd never feel truly safe again.

The stack of journals I'd brought from Florida caught my eye.

Untying the twine, I pulled a journal from the middle of the pile. The first few pages were similar to the journal I'd opened last night: equations and compounds.

On the third page, the writing was different. I didn't recognize it as my father's or grandfather's.

03/26/2015 – E.O.

Too recent to be my grandfather's.

We're almost ready to submit the proposal for human testing. The results with the lab rats were promising. Much like humans, a rat's amygdala processes emotions, fear, and aggression. LC and RC took a great deal of time indoc-

trinating the rats to associate a stimulus with fear. Some were made to fear loud noises. Some were frightened by bright or flashing lights. They even had some rats subject to fear of their feeder.

Utilizing automated segmentation techniques, their team utilized software algorithms to identify the activity of the amygdala, assessing true fear. After the first dose of $C16H21NO21$, when exposed to fear-triggering stimulus, the activity of the amygdala was reduced by over fifty percent.

Consecutive doses showed increased inactivity; however, not at the same rate.

The question I posed to our team was if the $C16H21NO21$ was the causative factor or if the repeated exposure to the stimulus was the reason for the decreased fear production.

Holy shit.

This was the early testing on what we now label Propanolol. The date was at least three years before Sinclair acquired the research.

I flipped through the pages, seeing more notes in the same handwriting.

Each entry began with a date and E.O.

The man Mom said was in the picture was Dr. Eric Olsen. I put his name into a search.

An announcement from Indianapolis University was one of the first articles to appear.

• • •

WE AT INDIANAPOLIS UNIVERSITY are saddened by the unexpected death of our distinguished and beloved professor emeritus Dr. Eric Olsen. His research with our university will forever be remembered. Originally from Detroit, Michigan, Dr. Olsen left behind a wife, Elizabeth (Weaver) Olsen, a daughter, Brenda Marie Olsen Carpenter (David), and three grandchildren. Donations in his name are being accepted.

"WHATEVER YOU'RE READING MUST BE interesting."

I gasped, bringing my hands to my chest. "Oh, you scared me."

In reality, Eli wasn't scary. He could be seen as intimidating, but that wasn't what I saw. The new rule-breaking side to my bodyguard was on full display. His crisp suit was gone, replaced by a black t-shirt that didn't completely cover the tattoos on his muscular arms, and low hanging blue jeans that hugged his sexy, firm ass.

Eli's gaze lingered, taking me in as his lips quirked into a sexy grin. "Did you forget about me already?"

"No," I said with a sigh. "I just..." I wasn't sure if it was important. "...found something in one of the journals from Dad's safe."

"What did you find?"

"Research notes about early testing on Propanolol, years before Sinclair acquired the research. There was a man in one of Dad's pictures who I didn't recognize.

Mom said his name was Eric Olsen. The notes all begin with the date and the initials E.O.”

“Why would your dad have those?”

I shrugged. “Honestly, I don’t know. In the notes, Dr. Olsen discusses early trials, failures and successes when the research was started at the university. He names researchers by initials: LC and RC.” I had an idea. “Maybe Dr. Carpenter brought the notes to Sinclair when he came to work for us.”

“How would Dr. Carpenter get Dr. Olsen’s notes?”

“Oh,” I said, standing. “Mom said Dr. Carpenter was married to Dr. Olsen’s daughter, Brenda.”

Eli’s brow furrowed. “I don’t know if that’s connected to what happened to your father.”

My phone on the desk vibrated. Eli came closer as I picked it up.

“It’s Damien.”

He shook his head. “Don’t answer.”

“I have to answer. He’ll worry.”

“I came to tell you something I recently learned. You can call him back after that.”

“Damien is not guilty of killing our father.”

Eli took the phone from my hand and swiped the red icon. “Listen to me first.”

Crossing my arms over my breasts, I stared incredulously at him. Despite his incredibly handsome face and toned body, I wasn’t a fan of being told what to do. “Talk.”

“The initial forensics came back on your dad’s

letter. Multiple latent fingerprints were found. None belonging to Derek Sinclair."

What?

I staggered backward, my knees folding as I fell to my chair. "None?"

Clenching his jaw, Eli shook his head. "They're running the prints through the government databases. Not everyone has fingerprints on file. In the state of Indiana, attorneys are required to submit their fingerprints as part of the bar admission process."

"Attorney. Stephen Elliott's fingerprints are on Dad's letter?"

"Yes. Do you recall last year when Damien had Darius arrested?"

"Yeah, Darius was broadcasting family laundry from in front of Sinclair Pharmaceuticals' main office building."

"Darius's fingerprints are on file," Eli replied.

"Were his on the letter?"

"No, but there were some with enough similarities to infer that they were from someone related to Darius."

"Not Dad?"

"Not Derek. Damien."

"No." I shook my head. "You're not sure, right? You said infer."

Eli squatted near my legs, laying his hand on my knee. "We need to get Damien's fingerprints to rule him out."

I met Eli's green stare. "Are you just going to ask him? He'll think you're a lunatic."

"Deidra can get them for us. She's currently in Damien and Ella's home."

"Dad and Damien worked together before Dad's retirement. Damien could have touched a piece of paper."

My phone vibrated again.

"I have to answer this."

"Don't tell Damien what you just learned."

"If he spoke to Mom, he knows I left Florida."

With his firm lips pressed together, Eli nodded.

My stomach twisted as I lifted the phone, hitting the green icon. My eyes met Eli's as I tried to hide the trepidation in my voice. "Hey."

TWENTY-SIX

Eli

Under normal assignment circumstances, I would have left Dani alone to talk to her brother. These weren't exactly normal circumstances. While I would have preferred if she put the call on speaker, I gathered from the way her jaw was set, I was pushing my luck.

Going to the window, I gazed down at the busy streets. There was a monster truck something or other happening at Lucas Oil and an Indiana Pacers game at Gainbridge Fieldhouse. The rest of the city was walking around as if the woman I loved wasn't in danger.

From the one-sided conversation, I could construe

the part I wasn't able to hear, but that wasn't the same as hearing it. It's like inferring the fingerprints are Damien Sinclair's.

When I heard Dani say goodbye, I turned back to her.

Since we'd returned from Florida, she'd changed her clothes to a loose-fitting sweatshirt and leggings that hugged her sexy legs. Her feet were bare, showing her pink toenails. Her hair was piled on top of her head in a messy bun. In a word, she was stunning.

"I suppose you want to know what he said," Dani said, standing.

"Speakerphone would have been nice," I said with a grin.

"You're pressing your luck."

I took a step toward her and reached out for her waist, tugging her hips toward mine. "You're my assignment, Dani. I need all the information to keep you safe."

"You can't make me think the worst about my brother. Damien and I have always been close. I was his best woman, like a best man, at his and Ella's wedding. Damien can be a pain in the ass, but he's not capable of taking a contract out on anyone, much less our father."

I placed my finger on her luscious pink lips. "Why did he call?"

"I was right. Mom told him I'd left Florida. She also told him that Stephen Elliott called her."

"Does Damien know why?"

"Mom said he was checking on her, and she thought it was sweet."

"Damien's thoughts?" I asked.

"He joked that Stephen will probably bill for the call."

"I could hear your end. You told him you came home early because you needed a break from thoughts of your father. That was good."

Dani's lips curled. "And you said I couldn't lie."

"I admit" —he kissed my nose— "you sounded convincing."

"The main reason for his call is Monday's executive board meeting. We need to fill Dad's seat. Stephen has been campaigning for us to bring on a man named Preston Ayers."

Titling my head, I repeated his name in my thoughts. "Why do I know that name?"

"If you spend much time in Indianapolis, you'd know him or of him. He's an arrogant ass if you ask me. He's also the top nominee for governor in the next round of elections. Our current governor can't run again due to term limits."

I took Dani's hand and led her out to the living room.

She stopped, her gaze going to the kitchen. "I know you won't drink wine, but I would like a glass."

"I'll have water."

"Come in the kitchen," she said with a grin. "I'm not an entitled assignment, and you're not an entitled bodyguard. We can both get our own drinks and come back out here."

"Tell me why Mr. Elliott is campaigning for Preston Ayers to be on the Sinclair executive board."

Dani freed a wineglass from the under-the-cabinet rack. Near the refrigerator was an already-opened bottle of cabernet. She removed the wine stopper. "I hope this is still good." She poured a small amount in her glass, swirled the deep-red liquid, and took a small sip. Her smile returned. "Still good." Opening a cabinet, she removed a tall glass and handed it to me. "Ice and water are in the refrigerator door."

Back in the living room, she turned on her fireplace.

"Cold?" I asked.

"The temperatures are dropping."

"I'll take it over the heat and humidity in Florida."

Dani laughed. "That was nothing. You should go down there in August."

The heat from the fire warmed the room, mostly illuminated by the flames and giving everything an orange glow. Dani stretched out her legs on the sofa. I lifted her feet, placing them in my lap as I sat. "I like being here with you."

"The feeling is mutual."

"You said you don't usually have mad, passionate sex on the second day."

Pink filled her cheeks. "I don't think that was exactly what I said."

"I may have added a few adjectives. Nevertheless"

—I laid my hand on her ankles— "how do you feel about the third day?"

"It depends."

I quirked my eyebrow. "On what?"

"Are you going to stay tonight or disappear after you think I'm asleep."

"You were asleep. I had work to follow up on." I sighed. "If I leave, it's because, you know, all great ideas come in the middle of the night."

"Or in the shower."

A laugh bubbled from my throat. "Another good option. Anyway, if it's okay with you, if I leave, I'll come back to your bed."

"That's definitely okay with me."

"What are you going to do?" I asked.

Dani took a sip of her wine. "About?"

"The executive board. Why would a politician be a good fit for Sinclair Pharmaceuticals' executive board?"

"Stephen sent over Preston's curriculum vitae." She swayed her shoulders. "He used to be the dean of research at Indianapolis University. He has his MD and a PhD in pharmacological research."

"Impressive."

"In my opinion, Preston only wants a seat on the board to further pad his resume. It will show the people of Indiana that he is interested in maintaining state businesses."

"Would it be a conflict of interest?"

Dani thought for a moment. "I'd need to check, but

as long as we're not receiving any state funds, there wouldn't be."

Staring into the flames, I had a thought. "Where did you say Eric Olsen carried out the early tests on Propanolol?"

"I'm not sure if I did. He worked at Indianapolis University. They began their research years before Damien found out about it. But it was shut down. Possibly because of Eric Olsen's death." She shrugged and after having a drink, set her glass on the coffee table. "I hadn't thought about that before, but maybe Preston worked with Dr. Olsen."

I made a mental note to check that.

Dani laid her head back. "I need to go grocery shopping tomorrow. How do you feel about delivery tonight?"

"You don't need to wow me with your cooking skills. I'm already impressed with you."

"My grandmother said the way to a man's heart is through his stomach."

Running my palm over Dani's legs, I squeezed. "I tried to get you out of my heart and mind many times over the last year. I've given up."

Dani sat forward, reaching for my hand. "You haven't been here long, but it feels like you never left."

I lifted her hand and kissed her knuckles. "What should we order?"

"Mexican."

TWENTY-SEVEN

Dani

Eli offered to clean up our containers after dinner. While he did that, I made my way back to my office. Sitting at my desk, I reopened the email with Preston Ayers's CV. The research notes that I assumed were from Dr. Olsen were dated 2015. According to Preston's CV, he wasn't employed by Indianapolis University until early 2018.

I tried to establish a timeline. The university website had a list of past and present deans. Preston took over after an interim dean, a Ralph Phillips. Prior to Phillips, Eric Olsen was the dean of research.

A quick check to be sure Eli wasn't near, and I called my brother. Damien answered on the second ring. "Dani."

"I have a quick question for you."

"Shoot."

Watching the doorway, I leaned back against my soft chair. "I'm looking into Preston Ayers. Didn't the original research for Propanolol come from Indianapolis University?"

"Yes. We acquired the early research in '18."

"We paid the university for the research?"

Damien cleared his throat. "The university had completely shut down their research. I'd already made our interest known. They hadn't gotten a patent. It was simply intellectual property."

"Who did we pay?"

"What difference does this make?" he asked.

"Ayers was the dean of research in '18."

"He wasn't in on the original research. It was shut down before he was appointed dean."

"It still seems odd that he now wants on our executive board." I had more questions. "Did Dad pay someone off for the formula? Was David Carpenter in on it?"

"David believed in what his father-in-law created. The market was wide open. David needed the funding and facilities to conduct further research and development. The university had no intention of continuing what it had started. Sinclair provided David with the means to complete the research and development." Damien took a breath. "Jack Webb mentioned that you got into Dad's safe. What did you find?"

"You were in it after Dad was shot."

"That entire week is a blur. You're right. Stephen and I got into it to find Dad's insurance policies. We didn't go through everything. I figured you and I would do that with Mom. Fuck, at that point, we weren't sure she'd make it."

"I'm sorry. I should have waited for you. It was after Eli and I discovered the journals missing from his desk that I wanted to find out if things were missing from the safe." I grinned. "Grandma's necklace was in there."

"The one Sharlene wanted?"

"Yeah. Mom should sell it if money is an issue."

Yes, I was fishing.

"No, it meant more to Dad since it was his mother's. Why would money be an issue? It can keep collecting dust. What journals were missing?"

"All the ones in Dad's desk. The drawer is completely empty."

"The fuck?" Damien questioned. "Did you alert the Sumter County Sheriff?"

"Eli is working on it."

"Hey, I should have told you that Eli was coming back. Everything since Dad's murder has been hard to keep straight."

"I was shocked to see him, but all is good now."

Eli stepped through the door, his eyebrows arching in a questioning manner.

"Speak of the devil." I spoke to Damien. "I need to go. I'm still not sure about Ayers."

"We can talk tomorrow. It's good you're back. We need to be united before the meeting on Monday."

"Bye." I disconnected the call and met Eli's green stare.

"Damien called again?"

"Did I say it was Damien?"

"No, but who else would you be discussing Ayers with. Plus, when I saw you, you were putting off guilty vibes."

I stood and made my way to him, craning my neck to keep his green gaze in sight. "I'm not guilty. I called him, not the other way around. I had a question. It doesn't concern what happened to Dad, but something we were talking about with Preston Ayers."

"Did Damien have an answer?"

Inhaling, I shrugged. "Not completely. I realized that Preston Ayers was the dean of research when Sinclair acquired the research on Propanolol. I asked Damien if Sinclair paid Indianapolis University for the right to research Propanolol. He said the university had shut down its research. The formula was not patented. It was simply intellectual property that came with David."

"David Carpenter who died after Sinclair received the patent."

"Eric Olsen was the dean of research while they were studying the formula, and he was killed. According to Mom, he was shot on a park bench in broad daylight."

"And now your father."

I swallowed the lump in my throat. "Five or more years later. Why now? This can't have anything to do with Dad's death."

"It seems like a lot of people ended up dead who worked on Propanolol."

"I worked with David. I'm still alive."

Eli's warm hands came to my waist, his long fingers splaying beneath my sweatshirt. "You're going to stay that way."

"Only for the next fifty or sixty years."

His touch moved upward until his eyes opened wide. "Well, Dr. Sinclair. It seems you forgot to put on a bra when you changed your clothes."

"I didn't forget. They're torture contraptions." I ran my palm over his soft t-shirt, feeling his hard chest. "Men don't have to wear a band around their chest with underwire pinching them all day long."

A laugh rumbled from his chest. "If the chemistry and science thing ever gets old, you should work for a lingerie company. I'm sure that description would enhance bra sales."

"I love chemistry and science. Solving a murder is more stressful."

Eli leaned down, bringing his lips to mine. "You shouldn't be trying to solve a murder. That's my job."

"I like your other job better."

"Which is?" he asked.

"Distracting me."

He arched an eyebrow as his cheeks rose. "Are you done in here for today?"

I looked back at my desk littered with Dad's journals and other papers. My monitors illuminated the area behind the desk. "Nothing that can't wait for tomorrow."

He tugged on my hand. "Then you should get some sleep."

My head shook. "No. Distracting first. Sleep second."

Through the living room, Eli stopped to check the lock on the front door, probably for the fifth time since our dinner was delivered. I turned off the fireplace. With my hand in his, we made our way to the primary bedroom. My king-sized bed was large for one person, the idea of sharing it made me smile.

Words weren't needed. We'd talked a lot. Not about personal things, but it seemed talking led to discussions related to Dad's death. This time was not to rehash what we knew, but to put that all aside.

Eli lifted my sweatshirt over my head, his laser green gaze going to my breasts which grew heavier with each passing second. "You should never keep them bound up."

"When you're a double D, there isn't much choice."

"Doubly delicious," he said with a gleam to his eye before bending at the waist and sucking one nipple and then the other.

My head lobbed back as I concentrated on the electric sensation. The energy wasn't contained to his fingers splayed on my ribs or where his mouth teased my nipples. It ricocheted from nerve ending to nerve ending, small explosions detonating beneath my skin.

Step by step, we moved until my legs collided with the bed.

Eli lay me back, reached for the waist of my yoga pants, and pulled them down past my ankles. As he reached for my panties, I sat up, tugging the hem of his black shirt. His bicep flexed as he helped pull it over his head.

"Jeans next," I said with a grin.

"Bossy."

"I can be."

His sexy grin twitched as he unbuttoned the top of his blue jeans and lowered the zipper. As the denim fell to the floor, he kicked off his loafers and stepped from the pants. "Now we're even."

Memories of last night added fuel to the heat smoldering within my veins. I slipped from the bed to the floor, landing on my knees. My line of sight was the large bulge beneath his boxer briefs.

"Fuck, Dani," he said, his voice an octave lower than seconds before.

I looked up through my hooded eyelids as my breathing quickened. "I want to taste you."

His nod was almost imperceptible, but it was the low growl and the way his nostrils flared that let me know he wasn't about to stop me.

Licking my lips, I reached for his waistband and pulled the silk fabric down to the floor. I'd felt the girth of him last night, but this was my first visual. The sight of his hardened cock with veins popping to life and precum glistening at the tip made me squirm as my core clenched. Reaching with one hand, I stroked the velvety surface, aware that my thumb and middle finger couldn't touch. Opening my lips, I took the head into my mouth. The salty, musky scent matched his taste. Up and down, I ran my hand and lips. Each time taking a little more and a little more.

"Fuck, you're killing me," he said as he reached for my hair.

I gasped as he fisted my loose bun and moved me, pulling me to him as his penis teased the back of my throat. Over and over, the pace grew faster. I held onto his thick thighs for support as his warm seed streamed over my tongue.

Kissing and licking, I swallowed all that he gave.

When I looked up, the desire in his gold-flecked orbs rattled my world.

Eli offered me his hand. "I wasn't expecting that."

"I'm a little rusty," I said as I stood.

"You're fucking amazing. Now, my turn."

CHAPTER
TWENTY-EIGHT

Dani

When I awoke Sunday morning, I expected to be alone. While it was only a little after six in the morning, Eli was still present, his breathing steady. I wasn't certain if he'd been up and working throughout the night. By the time I closed my eyes for the night, Eli had kept his word, his tongue, lips, teeth, and hands all working in tandem to bring me to an earthquaking orgasm.

That wasn't the end.

We lay for a while, his arm around me, and talked. For the first time, it wasn't about Dad or his murder. It wasn't about Sinclair Pharmaceuticals. He asked me more personal questions.

What was my favorite color?

How old was I when I knew I wanted to be a chemist?

Favorite childhood memories?

It was refreshing and intimate. Sometimes, I'd recount stories as I lay with my shoulder and face on his hard chest, swirling his chest hair with my fingers.

It wasn't all one-sided. I asked Eli questions, too.

At first, he seemed reticent to give more than a few-word answers, but in time, he opened up. He told me about his decision to join the military. His father had been a marine. Eli felt compelled to follow in his footsteps. Guardian Security came after his final tour. He said he hadn't been looking for security work to be his profession; Benjamin Clark sought Eli out.

He'd been with Guardian for nearly ten years.

A question I'd never before thought to ask came up. I asked how old he was.

Elijah Rhodes was eight years my senior.

Looking him in the eye, I giggled, telling him he was the oldest man I'd ever slept with. That was apparently the encouragement he needed to show me that he definitely wasn't too old. That round was slower with more touching, but the climax didn't disappoint as we came together, filling the air with our sounds of pleasure.

"Good morning," Eli said, rolling and covering me with his arm.

I wiggled my behind against his front. "Good morning."

"If you keep doing that, I don't think I'm going to allow you to leave this bed."

"Allow me?"

He nodded, his warm breath blanketing my neck as kisses peppered my shoulder.

With his morning erection probing my lower back, I didn't want to leave the bed.

I gasped as Eli shifted my legs, impaling my pussy. Arching my back, I wiggled to accommodate his size as his hands caressed my breasts. His rhythm began slow and gentle. In and out. As the speed increased, so did his ferocity. The friction brought my body to life as the heat within me built.

I couldn't think of a better way to start a day.

We rolled until I was up on my knees. The room filled with primitive sounds, noises that men and women have been making since Adam and Eve. High notes from me and baritone notes from him. They were our chorus, the refrain that one could listen to forever and always.

My orgasm came like the building of a pressure cooker. Higher and higher until I collapsed onto my stomach, Eli falling to my side. I lifted my head, meeting his green gaze for the first time this morning. "I was surprised to find you still in bed."

He kissed my nose. "You're hard to leave."

"I think you were the one who was hard."

"I was," he said with a grin. "And you are soft." He ran his palm down my spine and over my behind.

Closing my eyes, I exhaled. When I opened them, Eli was still looking at me. "What?"

"Ben told me something the other day. He said to listen to my gut."

"Is your gut telling you something?"

"It's telling me that I'm in way over my head with you. I don't know what you want."

I sat up, pulling the sheet over my breasts and feeling my well-fucked core. My lips pursed in a grimace.

"You can always say no," he said, watching my expression.

"I never doubted that." My hand cupped his cheek. "If I ever want to say no, I will. As for what I want..." I inhaled. "I want Dad's killer found, and if I'm completely selfish, I want this, you and I together, every night and every morning."

Eli laid his hand over mine and tugged it down. Intertwining our fingers, he lifted my hand and kissed my knuckles. "I don't think any of that sounds selfish."

"But it is," I admitted. "Last night you told me about your career with Guardian Security. If you're someone else's bodyguard, you would be with them, not me."

"Dani, I've never been *with* an assignment before. You said you don't sleep on the second day. I don't fuck my assignments. I'm not sure what the future holds, but I'd like to explore it openly. Guardian has other positions, people behind the scenes."

"I can't ask you to give up your passion. You're not

asking me to walk away from Sinclair Pharmaceuticals."

"Passions change." He leaned back against the headboard, the sheet slipping to his hips, a trail of dark hair disappearing just under the cover. "My passion was the Marine Corps and then Special Ops. I enjoy most of my assignments."

"Not all?"

He shook his head. "Not all. I've lived rather frugally over the last ten years and have been paid well. I'm sure I'm not as well-off as your family, but I'm hardly a pauper. I could spend some downtime and figure out what's next." He again reached for my hand. "I don't want us to move too fast and frighten one of us away."

"It's fast and it's slow."

He leaned over, kissing my cheek. "I understand completely."

I sat forward. "I'll shower and then...I think I have some eggs and bread. I can put together some kind of breakfast."

"Coffee?"

My lips curled. "Definitely coffee."

A few minutes into my shower, the bathroom door opened. Through the steam on the glass doors, I watched as Eli entered wearing only his boxer briefs and set a coffee cup on the vanity. "Um," I said, "thank you."

"Cream, no sugar." He slid the glass barrier and

scanned me up and down. "If I wasn't waiting on a phone call, I'd consider joining you."

"It may be difficult to do your job if you're too distracted."

"No. You'll remain safe. The alternative isn't an option." One more scan and Eli shut the shower door.

I didn't dry my hair, but I dressed in comfortable clothes, a teal green sports bra and leggings, covered by a wide-neck top. The morning sky was crystal blue as I opened the blinds in the bedroom. The sidewalks below were nearly empty, a big difference from last night. In the kitchen, I found not only eggs and bread, but bacon.

Once everything was cooked and warm, I walked down the hallway to Eli's office. It was also his bedroom; however, I had high hopes the bed would go unused. He was standing at the window, with his phone to his ear.

"Breakfast," I said softly.

Eli spun toward me. There were now blue jeans covering his boxer briefs but no shirt. I stared at his fit torso and wide shoulders. The smile and shimmering gaze from before were gone. If I were to evaluate, I'd say he looked angry.

"What happened?" I asked.

His Adam's apple bobbed. He nodded. "Keep looking into it," he said into the phone. "Let me know as soon as you have an answer." He disconnected the call. "Two handwriting experts agree that your father wasn't the person who wrote that letter."

"No." I furrowed my brow. "I know my own father's handwriting."

"It was similar. Whoever wrote it did a very good job of trying to imitate it. The experts look at more precise markers. The places where there's more pressure. While it's consistent in the letter, it's inconsistent with other handwriting samples they used for comparison."

"So, someone forged a note that basically sounded like Dad knew he was in danger. Why?"

"To throw us off."

I shook my head. "That's stupid. The note made us want to look more. What about the FBI guys?"

"It's connected. It's all connected." He quirked his lips. "Did you say breakfast?"

"I did. I really need to grocery shop."

We began walking toward the kitchen. "Can you have them delivered?"

"I mean, I can, but I'd like to get out."

"Give me until tomorrow. I want to keep working on some leads."

We sat at the breakfast bar. "Okay. I'll have them delivered." I picked up my phone. "I have a text message from Damien." I looked up at Eli. "He's on his way over. He wants to talk about Preston Ayers."

TWENTY-NINE

Eli

"Why did you change clothes?" Dani asked, looking up from her computer screen.

My comfortable attire was replaced by a black suit. "Your brother is paying for a bodyguard."

Dani's sexy smile grew as she stood and came closer. Her navy eyes swirled with multiple shades of blue, the churning of a turbulent sea. She reached for the lapels of my suit coat, pushed up on her tiptoes, and brought her lips to mine. "Are you saying that I can't do that when Damien is here?"

"Probably not." My hands went to her waist as I

held her at arm's length. "I want to talk to Damien for a few minutes."

Dani pursed her lips. "You're not going to accuse him of killing Dad."

"I don't intend to accuse him. I simply have some questions that I hope he can answer."

"Like what?"

Letting go of her waist, I contemplated what I could or should say. Ben's call divulged more than the information about the handwriting.

When my gaze met hers, Dani placed a fist against her hip. "Eli, there are many things I value in a relationship. It doesn't matter if it's a friendship, a sexual relationship, or what I share with my brother. Above all, the most important is honesty. This morning you talked about where this" —she motioned between the two of us— "is going. I want it to go beyond your assignment. However, I don't care how great the sex is, I have to trust that you'll be honest with me."

"You've accused me of wrongfully thinking the worst of Damien. You're right. The facts keep piling up in a way it's difficult to overlook."

"What facts?"

"He and the attorney opened your dad's safe."

"To find Dad's will and insurance papers."

"They had access to place the damning letter we found."

She crossed her arms over her breasts. "I spoke to Damien about the safe. He'd forgotten he'd even opened the safe."

"The latent fingerprints on the letter."

"Have they confirmed they're Damien's?"

I shook my head. "Not yet. That's one of my questions, to ask him for a fingerprint sample. Also, he had access to your and your parents' electronics. The virus was being sent to the Indianapolis area."

"Again, nearly two million other possibilities. And they were on his electronics too."

"A good way to throw us off."

I inhaled.

"Okay, the most damning is a recent five-million-dollar withdrawal from his crypto account."

Her arms dropped to her side. "A five-million-dollar withdrawal, when?"

"Ten days before your father was shot."

Taking two steps, I moved closer, cupping her soft cheek. "Dani, you wanted honesty. That's the God's honest truth. I asked Ben to run a check on Darius's and Damien's financials. Guardian didn't even know about Damien's crypto account last year. I'm not sure if he had it and we missed it, or it's new. The point is that he took half of the value from the account."

Dani took a step back. "I can't believe what you're saying."

"You don't want to believe it. There's a difference."

"No." She shook her head. "Let's think this through. Did Damien reinvest it somewhere?"

Inhaling, I nodded. "I didn't ask. Maybe Damien can shed some light on the subject."

The uncertainty in her blue orbs caused my chest

to ache. I wanted to take that doubt away and give her back the life she had—no, more than that, the life we could have together.

The ring of her doorbell echoed through the condominium.

"You can ask questions," she said matter-of-factly, "but I'm going to be present. I want to hear what he says."

I nodded. "Let me answer the door."

"You don't honestly think Damien is going to pull a gun on me in my own home."

I didn't think he would. I was more concerned that he wasn't the person who would show. Removing my gun from the holster, I walked to the door, ready to meet face-to-face with our FBI frauds.

"Eli," Damien said. His gaze quickly moved to the gun in my lowered hand and back to me. "What the hell?"

"You hired him," Dani said jokingly, coming from behind me. "We're a bit on edge."

"Why, has something new happened?"

Dani led her brother inside. "My refrigerator is pretty bare. Can I get you anything to drink?"

"No, I've already had too much coffee," Damien said, watching as I secured my gun in my holster. "Tell me what has you unnerved."

Dani sat on the sofa where last night she'd had her feet in my lap. Damien took a chair near the window, leaving me to either sit with Dani or opposite Damien. I chose the latter.

"We had some excitement in Florida," Dani began. She went on to tell him about the FBI men who visited the villa.

To his credit, Damien seemed rightfully appalled and concerned. He turned to me. "You reported them, right?"

I shook my head. "No. I didn't want to tip them off that we knew they were impostors."

"Well, fuck, Dani. No wonder you came home a day early." He leaned back, crossing his ankle over his knee. "I don't get it. You said someone took all of Dad's journals from his desk but didn't take anything from his safe."

"We thought maybe they didn't know about the safe until we opened it. As for missing, I don't know if anything was missing," Dani said. "I just know it contained items."

"Where are the contents you found?"

Dani pointed to the hallway with her office and my assigned bedroom. "I brought it all home. I've been going through the journals..."

Fuck, I wished that my earlier declarations would have caused her to be more cautious with what she was sharing. As she stood, I wanted to stop her. It was too late; she offered to show Damien what we'd discovered.

I followed the two of them a step behind, seething as they entered her office.

"...here are the journals we found in the safe," she said, pointing to the stack on her desk. "And in here"

—she lifted the blue and white striped bag— "are the other things."

Damien reached for the bag and lifted it to Dani's desk.

"We've been wearing gloves when we touched anything," Dani said, looking at me.

I pulled two pairs from my pocket. "Here you go."

"Why?" Damien asked.

I was the one to answer. "Someone from Guardian is coming later today to dust everything for prints. We want to know who had access to his safe."

"We did," Damien said, nodding his head to Dani. "Mom and Dad did."

"And Elliott," Dani said.

Damien's eyebrows came together. "He didn't know the combination. I opened the safe for him."

Dani spoke. "I thought you didn't remember opening it."

He shrugged. "I didn't until you reminded me."

"Did you find what you were looking for?" I asked.

"Stephen wanted to be sure Dad didn't have an old version of his will. There was a clause about selling Sinclair that was removed when Dad's will was redone last year."

"Was there an old version?" I asked.

Damien shook his head. "We cleared the whole thing out. The only thing we found that was relevant at the time were his life insurance policies." He turned to Dani. "As I recall, you were at the house with us."

She wrinkled her nose. "I don't think I was. I don't remember the two of you going through the safe."

"No," he said. "You were at the hospital with Mom. I remember because you called me to tell me she was out of surgery."

"You cleared out the safe?" I asked. "So your fingerprints will be found on all of that." I pointed to the bag.

"Yeah, I suppose. Mine and Stephen's. Once we found what we needed, we put everything back. I locked it up and forgot about it until recently."

Covering his hands with the gloves, Damien reached into the bag. The box clanked with the sound of coins. He grinned. "Dad loved his coin collection."

One by one, he removed things from the bag and placed them on Dani's desk.

"Do you see anything new?" she asked. "Or is anything missing that you recall."

"Like I said that whole trip is a blur." He stared at the contents. "I think there was a photo album."

"I left that with Mom," Dani volunteered.

"This trip down memory lane is nice," Damien said, "but Dani and I need to discuss the executive board meeting tomorrow."

Her blue gaze met mine. "Eli can stay."

"No offense," Damien said, "but it's a private matter."

"None taken." I crossed my arms over my chest and leaned against the wall. "Forget I'm here."

"Dani," Damien protested.

CHAPTER
THIRTY

Dani

"Will Grace be back by tomorrow?" I asked. Damien nodded, his dark blue eyes still on Eli.

"Hey. Eli is just doing his job. Talk to me about Preston."

Damien's stance relaxed. He pulled the latex gloves from his hands and dropped them in the trash can. "If we're all going to discuss this, let's go back out to the living room. It's a little close in here."

Damien led the way. When I looked up at Eli, I had the feeling he was still suspicious of my brother. If anything, what was just said made me feel less suspect.

Damien admitted to touching everything in the safe. He remembered the photo album, and he never mentioned the letter. That meant he didn't know about it.

The letter was hidden under the felt at the bottom of the safe. When he and Stephen cleared it out, they probably didn't look beneath the felt.

Back in the living room, we retook our seats.

Damien inhaled and leaned forward, putting his elbows on his knees. "Stephen thinks Ayers is a good fit. He'll bring a new level of prestige to the executive board, and he has some thoughts on future endeavors. Stephen also thinks we should encourage Mom to retire from the board."

What?

I sat taller. "And replace her with who?"

"You."

"Me." I blinked. "I..." I didn't know what to say.

Damien sat taller. "Think about it, Dani. You should have been on the board years ago. With Dad gone, Mom doesn't want or need the pressure of Sinclair Pharmaceuticals. You on the other hand are part of the everyday workings. You know more than anyone on the board about how Sinclair operates."

My gaze went to Eli and back to my brother. "I know a hell of a lot more than Preston Ayers."

Damien scoffed. "You do."

"If Preston is such a good fit, why didn't his name come up when Gloria Wilmott stepped down?" I asked.

"Dad and Preston didn't see eye to eye on a litany of subjects."

I furrowed my brow. "Like what?"

Damien's eyes went to Eli and back to me.

"Everyone from Guardian signs an NDA," I said. "Whatever you have to say, you can say it in front of Eli."

"It's old hat," Damien said. "It doesn't matter now. What matters is that we walk into the meeting tomorrow ready to put this dark chapter behind us and move forward. Our stockholders need to see that we're progressing. What I'm about to say makes me sound like an ass, but I'm going to say it. If we go in there and propose adding you to Dad's seat, despite your overqualifications, there are people who will scream nepotism."

He did sound like an ass, but he was right.

"Preston Ayers in Dad's seat will show our willingness to grow. You in Mom's seat will then be better accepted."

"Have you talked to the other members of the board," I asked.

"Art Hatfield and Lynwood Sharp are on board."

"Grace, Rachel, and Phillip McGee?"

Damien responded, "Grace is getting up to speed. Rachel is a probably, and Phillip has only been on the board since Gloria retired. I don't think he'll put up too much resistance."

"Have you discussed this with Darius?"

Damien stood. "Fuck no. He owns shares of Sinclair stock. That's where his involvement ends."

"You know he'd like to be on the board."

"Not fucking going to happen." He turned toward the tall windows.

I remembered something Damien said before dropping the bomb of putting me on the board. "What ideas does Ayers have for the future of Sinclair?"

Damien turned around. "The pharma coalition Ella heads has helped. The prescription rate of Propanolol has increased significantly. Ayers believes it could do better. He wants to create a PR campaign aimed at veterans. I see the potential."

"I thought your plan was to spend more money on R&D, fewer payouts to stockholders, and less money on advertising."

"It was. The bottom line could use some help."

"So you're going to spend money to make it?"

He nodded. "That's the way it works."

I pressed my lips together. "Ayers wants Sinclair to do a PR campaign aimed at veterans. I can see that as a way to aid his campaign for governor."

Damien exhaled. "It could be mutually beneficial."

"Problems? You never said there were problems."

"Not problems, Dani. Forks in the road. And now with Dad gone, I'm willing to try something new."

I stood, meeting my brother. "Why did you cash out your crypto?"

His gaze narrowed. "The fuck?"

"Why?"

"Stephen advised that the crypto market is too unstable and uncertain. I'd made some decent profits and with the way the economy is going, I decided to put that money into a more secure venture."

"You reinvested it?"

"I did."

"In what?"

"Sinclair Pharmaceuticals."

I blinked. "You put five million of your own money in Sinclair Pharmaceuticals?"

Damien looked at Eli and back to me. "I'm not sure how you know that, but yes."

Eli stood. "Can you produce the receipts?"

My brother squared his shoulders. "I can. I don't need to. What the actual fuck?"

I stepped between the two men. "Those fake FBI agents, Damien. They were hired by someone. We hypothesize that they were hired by the same person who paid for Dad's murder."

"Do you have proof that someone paid for his murder?"

"No," I admitted.

"When you get it, take it to the fucking police. Let them do their job." He turned on Eli. "Your job was to keep my sister safe and defend her from danger, not fill her head with unfounded ideas." His blue eyes were back on me. "Do you think I could or would have anything to do with Dad's murder?"

Tears prickled the back of my eyes. "I don't want to."

"I loved Dad. I fucking respected him. It's one of the reasons I wouldn't bring up Preston Ayers to him. I knew he'd freak out."

"Why would he freak out?"

Damien took a deep breath. "I don't know."

"What do you mean you don't know?"

My brother ran his hand over his dark-blond hair. "I didn't ask questions. Dad said it was better that way."

"Shit, Damien. What are you talking about? This could be why Dad is dead."

"No," he said adamantly. "What I'm referring to happened too long ago. Johnathon and Ella are working on the connection to our products. There's a pending wrongful death case in Georgia. The family claims their 82-year-old father died from an allergic reaction to Sinclair Pharmaceuticals' saline during surgery."

"Saline allergies are rare."

Damien nodded. "I called the Sumter County Sheriff's Department yesterday with the information. They're going to look into it."

"If the patient had an allergy, it was up to them to disclose it. The anesthesiologist would be responsible, not Sinclair."

"I know that," Damien said. "Stephen said the same thing. People want to turn tragedy into a payday."

"What didn't you ask questions about?" Eli asked, stepping into the conversation.

My brother's shoulders slouched. "Fine. I was the one who discovered the research for Propanolol. The dean of the university wanted to raise money to fund the ongoing research."

"Eric Olsen?" I asked.

"No, his name was Oaks. Olsen was the dean of the research department. There were positive early results. I offered to buy their research, and my offer was turned down. I even tried to hire their scientists. When that didn't work, I told Dad about it. It was when Darius was busy shitting all over Sinclair. Dad was intrigued with the uniqueness of the formula. Things got complicated after the university shut down the research."

"Eric Olsen was killed, shot in broad daylight like Dad," I said.

Damien nodded. "The university wasn't giving up their results or even the formulas. The two main scientists disappeared. That's when I found David Carpenter. He knew about the research because he was Eric Olsen's son-in-law and had access to his personal notes."

My voice quivered with trepidation. "Did Dad do something illegal to encourage David to work for Sinclair?"

"Dani, this was over five years ago, hell, eight at this point. I don't know exactly what Dad did, but David recreated the formula. Our research was fast-tracked, and now Sinclair is a world competitor in the pharmaceutical world."

The pieces were falling into place. "Preston Ayers was the dean of research in '18. He's who made a deal with Dad, and you say Dad didn't like him. Why are we even considering adding him to the board?"

"Dad didn't include me in on the agreement for the research. I don't know what Dad's beef was with him."

"Stephen would know," I said. "Wouldn't he?"

"I don't think we should rehash any of this. If anything came out, it could reflect poorly on Sinclair."

I raised my voice. "It could find Dad's killer."

"Or," Eli said, "it could get the two of you killed." He looked at Damien. "Why haven't you hired yourself a bodyguard?"

Damien stood taller. "I don't need a bodyguard."

"But you hired one for Dani, your parents, and your wife."

"Because I don't want anything to happen to any of them."

"You're not worried about yourself?" Eli asked.

"I wasn't," Damien replied with a tilt of his head. "Now you have me concerned."

THIRTY-ONE

Eli

I turned to Damien. "Would you be willing to submit a fingerprint sample?"

"Of course." He pointed toward the hallway. "I touched the things in Dad's safe. I've told you that."

"It's just routine."

"Bullshit," Damien said. "You fucking suspect me. I'm the one paying you."

"Damien." Dani stepped closer. "If Guardian can eliminate our fingerprints, it could help them find who else was in the safe."

He lifted his palms to his temples. "You said whoever stole the journals didn't get in the safe. So what fingerprints are you trying to find?"

Dani looked at me, asking permission. If only she'd

done that earlier. I nodded. At this point, I wasn't certain what to think.

"Damien, we found one other thing in Dad's safe."

"What?"

"It was a letter written by Dad."

His blue eyes narrowed. "Let me see it."

"We don't have it," I replied. "I sent it to the main Guardian office. They ran it for prints. Derek's prints weren't on it."

"Then he didn't write it."

Dani and I nodded.

"Whose were?"

"Possibly yours," Dani said. "If you give a sample, we'll know for sure or eliminate you as a possibility."

"Fine," he said. "Take my prints. I don't have a fucking clue what you're talking about. There wasn't a letter when we cleared out the safe."

Dani replied, "It was in a manila envelope under the felt on the bottom of the safe."

Damien sat back in the chair. "Fuck, I can't remember if we looked there. I'd have to ask Stephen." He looked back up to both of us. "If it wasn't there, that means that someone put it in between the time we all went down when Dad was shot to when you found it. Has anyone else been in the house?"

"The people who took the journals," I said.

"But they didn't take the things in the safe. They came to you, knowing you had."

Dani nodded as she took a seat. "It's a circle. It doesn't make sense."

"Unless," I said, "those people planted the letter."

Dani met my gaze. "Why come to us about the contents of the safe? They brought attention to themselves."

I shrugged. "Maybe they thought you'd tell them what you found. They were confirming that we had the letter."

She shook her head. "It doesn't make sense."

"What did it say?" Damien asked.

"The handwriting looked like Dad's," Dani began. "But two handwriting experts from Guardian say it was forged." She took a breath. "I only read it once, but it said something about 'if we found the note, Dad's worst nightmare came true." She turned to me.

One of the skills of my profession was photographic memory.

"It said," I went on, *"If this is ever found, my worst nightmare came true. I pray it was only me that he came after and that those I love are safe. The decision wasn't easy, but given the circumstances, I would do it again. No price is too high to save that which was built. Don't question. Don't let the truth come out. I'll take it to my grave; let it rest there. Please, to those who know, keep your word, for the sake of my family and legacy."*

Damien slumped back in his chair. "Fuck."

"The thing is," Dani said, "if Dad didn't write it, who did and why?"

"Someone," Damien said, "wants us to question. If those fake FBI agents planted it, and then went to you, they must have wanted to know that you found it."

Dani looked my direction. "We didn't confirm or deny what we found. They wanted to see it, and you told them no."

My eyes opened wider. "There's one other way for them to confirm that we found it. If someone checks the safe and it's missing."

Her blue gaze sparkled. "Have you checked your new surveillance devices?"

"No," I said, turning toward my makeshift office.

Dani and Damien were on my tail as I went into the small bedroom and brought to life my desktop that Larry had set up. A few clicks and I had the program. I only set up the camera yesterday. Truthfully, the FBI guys could have gone back Friday night after talking to us. If that were the case, my camera was too late.

"The camera in the office picked up on motion yesterday afternoon," I said.

Dani and Damien came into the room, peering over my shoulder. We all stared at the screen as a small light-brown dog ran in circles on the floor. I'd only seen the dog once. I turned to Dani. "Is that Hoosier?"

With her eyes as wide as saucers, she nodded.

A woman's voice could be heard before she could be seen. Carol, Marsha's neighbor, spoke to the dog as she pulled back the picture frame and entered the correct code. She lifted the felt liner and placed it back. After relocking the safe and returning the picture frame, she turned to the dog. "That's good. I'll let him know they have it. Come on, Hoosier. Let's go home."

"Him," Dani said, turning to her brother.

"Not fucking me."

"Who?" When neither one responded, I asked, "What do you know about Carol?"

Damien shook his head. "Nothing."

Dani pursed her lips. "Her last name is Webster. Her husband passed away before she moved next door to Mom and Dad. Why she knew the combination to the safe, no clue." Her blue eyes opened wider. "Carol was the one to tell us about the people taking things from Mom's house. Why would she do that if she is working with them?"

Damien spoke. "Eli, can you find Carol's phone and see who she called last night? Was there a time stamp on that video?"

"I'll do my best."

Damien looked at his watch. "I need to get home to Ella and Dylan. Call me as soon as you learn anything." He and Dani walked toward the front door.

I followed, interested in what might be said.

"I'm sorry," Dani said as she reached for her brother's hand. "I never thought you were capable of hurting Dad."

"There was some interesting circumstantial evidence."

"Eli said to follow his gut. I followed mine. Mine said you couldn't do that."

"I couldn't, but I'm starting to believe he's not far off with the murder-for-hire theory." Damien kissed her cheek. "Stay safe."

She turned, seeing me standing in the hallway. "I'm safe."

Damien pointed at me. "Thirty minutes ago, I was ready to fire your ass."

"You can fire me right now. I'm not leaving Dani."

"Until you know she's safe?" he added.

"I'm not leaving period."

Damien looked at Dani and back to me with a shake of his head before exiting through the door. Once he was gone, Dani secured the lock and turned, her knowing grin on display. "I told you it wasn't him."

"I'm eighty percent certain you're right."

"Only eighty?" She came in my direction, and I met her halfway, my hands going to her waist and hers going to my shoulders. "You're not leaving?"

"No."

"You told Damien that."

"I did." I kissed her nose. "I'm fucking in love with you. I'm not going to fight it."

"You're in love with me?"

"Yes."

"I think I could be in love with you."

"You think?" I asked.

"Well, you were going to shoot my brother."

"No, I would only have shot if it hadn't been Damien at the door, but our FBI guys."

Dani took a step back, reaching out and holding my hand. "I never thought of that."

I tugged her back until she was flush against me.

"That's why I'm here. You don't need to worry. I've got it covered." I looked down at my suit. "I'm going to change back into my blue jeans and save this suit for tomorrow's executive board meeting. Then, I'm going to find out all I can about Carol Webster."

"I'm going to do more homework on Preston Ayers. If Dad didn't like him, I can't in good faith agree to have him on our board."

"Hey," I said, "if you're not currently a member of the executive board, how do you get a say?"

"I have Mom's proxy."

"What does she think about Ayers?"

Dani nodded. "I'm going to find out."

CHAPTER

THIRTY-TWO

Dani

Mom didn't answer the first or second time I called. Eli gave me Jack's number. He answered right away, telling me that Mom was in physical therapy, but he'd have her call once she was done.

The entire conversation with Damien and Eli played continuously through my thoughts. Every time we made a discovery, something about it felt off. How in the world could Carol Webster be involved in planting a forged letter in Dad's safe? Why?

My next call was to Stephen Elliott. He answered on the third ring.

"Dani, what an unexpected pleasure. What can I do for you?"

"I wanted to thank you for checking on Mom. She's lonely. Your call was nice."

"I was going to call you about that."

"What?" I asked.

"As you know, the Sinclair executive board will be meeting tomorrow. I checked in with Marsha to find out if she planned to vote via Zoom or proxy. She told me that you were her proxy."

"I am. Damien and I share her POA, too."

Stephen's voice lowered. "I hope you've spoken to Marsha about Preston Ayers."

The small hairs on the back of my neck came to attention. "I called her a little while ago to discuss him, and she is in therapy."

"Well, she's in favor," Stephen said. "Preston and Derek went way back. Preston was in our fraternity at Purdue."

"I didn't realize that."

"Oh yes. He has a great resume."

"I read his CV," I said. "Thank you for that. My question is why didn't Dad like him?"

"I don't know what you're talking about."

"Preston was never nominated for the board in the past when Dad was alive. I mean, if he's such a great candidate, why wasn't his name mentioned when Gloria resigned and Phillip was voted in?"

"I'm sure Preston was mentioned. You know he has a lot of obligations. Yes, I'm sure Derek and I spoke about him. It just wasn't the right time. Damien agrees."

"Damien and I spoke today." I paused. "Stephen, did Dad…" I wasn't sure how to phrase my question. "…was there a deal that Dad made with Preston Ayers regarding Propanolol?"

"What would make you ask that?"

"You were the head of Sinclair's legal department at the time. It seems to me that if a deal was made, you would have been involved."

"Propanolol has turned Sinclair around. There was the scientist…David Carter, I believe. He came to Derek. No, Damien found him. Preston wasn't part of the university when the primary research was conducted."

"You mentioned to me that you saw the journals in Dad's desk drawer."

"Yes," he replied. "I was looking for a copy of his old will."

"That's what you said. Are you sure it was the drawer where you looked or Dad's safe?"

"I couldn't access the safe."

"Damien could."

"I suppose so. We weren't all thinking straight. I hope you get ahold of Marsha and talk to her about Preston. I know she'd want you to vote her proxy for him."

"Thank you, Stephen. I need to go."

"I'll see you tomorrow at the meeting. Good night, Dani."

I disconnected the call.

Stephen acted like he didn't have access to the

safe, but Damien said he did, that they explored it together. I could talk to Eli, but if I did, he would go back to suspecting Damien. I wanted with all my heart to believe my brother.

Reaching for another of Dad's journals, I leaned back in my desk chair and began flipping through the pages of formulas. A loose page floated to my lap. Picking it up, I read what I believed to be my father's handwriting. The text was dated a year ago in the spring. That was around the time of his heart attack. Once I started reading, I couldn't stop.

No one will read this. I'm not writing it for it to be read. I'm writing to calm myself. I figured out who Carol Webster is. Webster was her second husband's name. She's Carol Carpenter, David Carpenter's mother. I can't tell Marsha. She wouldn't understand. Explaining it all to her would break her heart and I refuse to do that.

It wasn't until Carol was in my office and she saw the photo of Sinclair Pharmaceuticals that I realized she knew the connection. It was her comment in passing that made me worried. She mentioned her grandchildren. The name coincidence was too strong. I called the only one who knew what happened, Phen. He's never let me down.

He told me to play dumb.

How would I know a scientist who worked during my final years before retirement. Sinclair employs hundreds of people. Besides, there's no proof that David's illness was a result of his work for us. He'd been working for years with his father-in-law. Indianapolis University could easily be responsible.

That's how I procured Olsen's work, allowing David to continue the research. When Preston Ayers tried to stop our continuation of the research, I threatened him. I told him that if the research didn't continue, David would go public with the safety exposure he'd experienced.

It would ruin their research department. They'd lose funding and endure a long investigation. Hell, it was on shaky ground already with the disappearances of their scientists.

My blood pressure is down.

I needed to get that off my chest.

Hell, we paid David to keep us out of his story. We paid money we didn't have. It was worth it. Sinclair is stronger than ever. I saved it and I'd do it again.

My HANDS SHOOK as I laid the page on the desk.

With shaky knees, I made my way across the hallway to Eli.

He looked up, concern showing in his green orbs. "What's the matter?"

"I found something."

"Fuck, you look pale." He rushed to me, wrapping me in his arms.

"My dad," I said as tears punctuated my words. "He...come look."

Eli held my hand as we went back to my office. I lifted the piece of paper. "This fell out of one of the journals. Dad must have hidden it there. The date is a few days before his heart attack. I think this was the catalyst that caused it, the stress." I leaned against my desk and handed him the small piece of paper.

His eyes widened as he read. Once he was done, he met my gaze. "I'd just confirmed her first husband's last name. I hadn't put it together with your David."

"Damien didn't have Dad killed. Stephen did."

"Why do you say that?"

"In that note, he said he called Phen. That's the name Mom said Dad called Stephen ever since college. Stephen would have known that Carol was David's mother. He used her to help plant that fake note."

"What does Stephen gain from your father's death?"

"I want to ask him."

THIRTY-THREE

Eli

"No fucking way am I taking you to him. We contact the police."

"And say what, that my father did something horrible eight years ago that resulted in his death." She picked up the page. "This isn't enough evidence. We need more." She looked at me pleadingly. "I'll wear a wire. You can do that, can't you?"

I took a step back and lifted my arms over my head. "I'm not risking your life. If you're right, Stephen Elliott is capable of murder."

"He can't just shoot me in his house. You can come with me."

"No," I said. "I'll interview him for you."

Dani shook her head. "He won't tell you anything. I'm not sure he'll tell me. I have to try."

"Will he be at the board meeting tomorrow?"

"Yes," she said. "I can't wait until tomorrow. I must find out today." She turned toward the window. "It's still early. I just called him."

"You called him?" What the fuck?

"He said he spoke to Mom and Mom wants me to use her proxy to vote in favor of Preston Ayers."

"What did your mom say?"

"I couldn't reach her. Remember, I asked for Jack's number. He said she was in therapy. But Stephen said other things. He claimed to never have had access to Dad's safe."

"Damien said he did."

She nodded. "I know. That means Stephen is lying. Why?"

"Or Damien is."

"Stop it," she said louder than necessary. "Wait. Wait." She turned a circle. "You couldn't confirm Damien's fingerprints on the letter that Dad supposedly wrote, but you did say they found Stephen's on there."

I closed my eyes and exhaled. "You're right."

Dani reached for my arms. "Take me over to his house. He lives on the north side in the Butler-Tarkington area. I'll call him and let him know I want to talk to him about Ayers. He won't be suspicious."

"Fuck, I don't like this. Ask to meet him someplace public." I pulled out my phone and ran a quick search.

"There's a place called Meridian Restaurant & Bar on North Meridian. Ask him to meet you there."

"And you can set me up with a wire?"

My gut was telling me not to do this.

"Wait," she said. "If I can get him to say something, is it even permissible in court if he doesn't know he's being recorded?"

"Indiana is a one-party consent state. As long as one person, you, know you are recording, it's legal."

She bobbed her head. "Let's do this."

Fuck was playing on repeat in my head as I went over to the room with all the things from Larry. I wasn't even sure he'd brought me the equipment I needed. Out of the closet, I pulled a suitcase. Opening the clasps, I looked inside. There was a blue velvet bag. "Fuck, I was hoping I didn't have what we needed."

"But you do?" Dani questioned.

"Yes."

She squeezed my arm. "Eli, you'll be with me. Nothing will happen. I need to know what Stephen knows about David Carpenter and the deal Dad made. That note said that he paid David money he didn't have. Where did he get it?"

"I'm changing clothes again." I scanned her curves. "What about you?"

"I suspect the restaurant will want more than these yoga pants. I'll call Stephen and change."

As I closed my suit coat over my holster, Dani came into the bedroom. Her long hair was again piled on her head and her casual clothes were replaced by navy-blue slacks and a white blouse. "Stephen said he could meet me at Meridian Restaurant & Bar at five o'clock."

"I fucking wish there was another way to do this. Maybe you could call Damien."

Dani's expression fell. "Eli, I need to know that it's Stephen who's lying and not Damien."

The microphone I attached to Dani's bra strap was smaller than a penny. We tested it a few times and her voice came through my phone where I would record her conversation. "This has a decent range. If the restaurant is busy, that could make it more difficult to pick up his voice."

"I'll sit as close as possible."

I didn't like that either.

It didn't take long on a Sunday evening to reach the restaurant. I pulled the SUV around the log building and parked in the back lot. "Have you figured out what you're going to say?"

Dani tugged on her lip with her teeth. "I'm going to wing it."

"I won't be far away. If you need help, say the word and I'll be there."

I saw Stephen Elliott at Derek's funeral. As soon as we entered the restaurant, I spotted him sitting at a table for two along the wall next to the bar. His mostly gray hair was full and wavy. His expression was stoic until he saw Dani.

"I'll sit at the bar, where I can keep an eye on you."

Dani nodded as she walked toward the table. Her

voice came through my earbud and was recording on my phone. "Stephen. Thanks for meeting me."

"Let me flag down our waitress, and I'll get you a drink. You're a red wine drinker, right?"

"Good memory," she said, taking the chair across from him.

"What is it that you want to know about Preston?"

From my angle, I saw him point to a dish in the center of the table.

"I hope you don't mind. I ordered this charcuterie board. Help yourself."

Dani shook her head. Placing her arms on the edge of the table, she leaned forward. "No, thank you. I came to find out what deal Dad and Preston had regarding David Carpenter."

A waitress approached.

"The lady would like your best cabernet," Stephen ordered.

"Right away," she said and walked away.

"That wasn't necessary."

"I don't like to drink alone." He chuckled. "There wasn't a deal to my knowledge."

"There was," Dani said. "And you knew about it. I found proof. Is that deal what got Dad killed?"

"Danielle, I've known you all your life. You're a scientist, not someone prone to dramatic stories."

"David Carpenter was the son-in-law of Eric Olsen, the dean of the research department when Damien started trying to get his hands on the Propanolol research. Of course, it wasn't Propanolol yet. Eric Olsen was killed, and eventually Preston Ayers was named dean of research. David Carpenter was ill due to an exposure to what...chemicals, something to do with the research?"

"You really do have a vivid imagination. Here, have some brie cheese. It's delicious."

Dani continued, "Somehow, Dad convinced David to work for Sinclair. The research had been shut down by the university. Even though I was told it was intellectual property and not a patent, intellectual property is still protected by law. Sinclair Pharmaceuticals would have needed permission from the research department to allow us to research, develop, and manufacture Propanolol."

"You're asking questions that are better left buried."

"As in, buried with my father."

Stephen lowered his tone. "As in left alone."

The two sat straighter as the waitress delivered Dani's wine.

She didn't pick it up. "Dad paid David a lot of money. Where did he get it?"

"Sinclair is solvent."

"It is now," Dani said. "It wasn't back then. This all occurred during the 'dark Darius days.' You said that yourself the other day on our call."

"I really can't recall. It was years ago."

"Why now?" she asked. "Why have Dad killed now?"

"I suppose that's for the police to decide."

"You had a virus put on my technology and my parents'. It searched for keywords. What were you looking for?"

Stephen leaned back. "I understand you're dealing with a lot of things right now, Danielle, but these accusations..."

"Guardian Security traced the virus to your personal computer."

Now she's bluffing.

Stephen picked something off the charcuterie board and popped it into his mouth. "I'm an old man. I know nothing about those things."

"IP addresses don't lie. Virtual network made it harder to track but not impossible."

He brushed his hands over the table as his napkin fell to the floor. Stephen leaned down to pick it up, but Dani was faster. My eyes were on her as she lifted the napkin.

She handed it back. "Dad considered you his best friend."

"The feeling was mutual."

Dani lifted her glass of wine and took a hearty drink. "What did you gain from his death?"

"I lost a dear friend."

The sound of Dani's cough echoed in my ears.

"Oh, dear," he said, "your lips are blue."

Fuck.

As I rushed from the bar, Stephen Elliott whispered, "You shouldn't have been so noisy."

Dani reached for her throat as I pulled her from the

chair. I spotted the pecans right away. Her lips were pale, and her pulse was weak. I opened her lips to her swollen tongue. In the bottom of her glass, submerged in the wine, was a pecan.

"You son of a bitch. You tried to poison her."

"I don't know what's happening." Stephen stood. "Help. Someone call an ambulance."

"She's allergic to nuts."

THIRTY-FOUR

Eli

I paced outside the hospital room. It had been three hours since I injected Dani with the epinephrine. I'd read about her allergy a year ago, but it was her reminder yesterday on the plane that spurred me to locate and carry her EpiPen. The paramedics said that without the injection, she would be dead, just like the other people who worked on Propanolol.

The hospital room door opened. Damien and Ella Sinclair came out. Ella's eyes were red and puffy. She wrapped her arms around me. "Thank you. You saved Dani's life."

"Is she awake?"

"She's resting," Ella replied.

"Where's Stephen?" Damien asked, daggers shooting from his eyes.

"He left the restaurant, claiming he didn't know about her allergy."

Ella looked to her husband. "Did he know?"

"She's had it all her life. As close as he's been to our family, he fucking knew." Damien handed me back my phone.

"Did you listen?" I'd offered to let him hear Dani and Stephen's exchange.

Damien nodded with a clenched jaw.

"What are your thoughts?" I asked.

"I want Stephen Elliott to rot in prison for the rest of his miserable life."

"Before I gave you my phone to hear that recording, I contacted Ben. They're running a search of Elliott's financials. Dani hadn't lied about the trace of the virus, even though I bet she thought she had. Ben confirmed that the virus reported back to a virtual network that they've traced to Stephen's home."

Ella shook her head. "I can't believe it. Why?"

My phone vibrated. "It's Ben. Maybe we will learn more. Eli here," I said into the phone.

"We have a wealth of information."

I looked around the hallway and motioned for the Sinclairs to come closer. "Ben, I'm putting you on speaker."

"Speaker? Who is with you?"

"Damien and Ella Sinclair."

"First off," he said. "Carol Webster, formally

Carpenter, has been in contact with Stephen Elliott. The Sumter County Sheriff's department is on their way to pick her up for questioning."

"We'll need to get Hoosier," I said.

"I don't know what that means," Ben replied. "But have you heard of a man named Preston Ayers?"

"Yes." I met Damien's stare.

"Two months ago, Preston paid Elliott five hundred grand. Elliott turned around and gave three hundred grand as a campaign donation for Preston's upcoming gubernatorial election."

"What happened to the other two hundred?" Damien asked.

"We're working on the identity of the sender, but Carol Webster received a hundred thousand wire deposit around the same time. Another hundred was invested in cryptocurrency. That's more difficult to track."

"How does Ayers fit in?" Damien said.

"He wants to run for governor," I replied. "Whatever he and Derek did eight years ago, it's a story he didn't want to get out."

"Can we fucking prove this?" Damien asked.

"We're putting it together," Ben said. "Guardian has a good relationship with law enforcement. I'll put out a call to IMPD."

Damien turned to Ella. "We need to get word out. Tomorrow's meeting is postponed."

Damien shook my hand. "Did you mean what you said about sticking around?"

"If Dani will have me."

Ella grinned. "That's the best news to come out of this."

As the Sinclairs walked toward the elevator, I opened the door to Dani's room. Stunning blue eyes met mine as I walked toward the bed.

Dani reached for my hand. "Thank you." Her voice was scratchy.

"Doing my job."

"Is that all?"

Bending down, I kissed her forehead. "I fucking couldn't believe that he got to you with me right there."

"You saved me. If you hadn't had that EpiPen with you..."

I stroked her hair away from her face. "I'll never be without one again."

"What's happening with Dad's case?"

"Ben made financial connections between Elliott and Carol Webster and Elliott and Preston Ayers."

Dani's eyes opened wide. "Ayers?"

"It seems he pulled the strings. As a potential for governor, he wanted to keep the story about what happened years ago buried. He paid off Elliott and David's mother and silenced your dad."

A tear escaped her eye. "Dad never would have said a thing. He shouldn't be dead."

"Damien and Guardian Security will make sure they all pay."

"What if the story hurts Sinclair Pharmaceuticals?"

"I think your brother can handle whatever comes."

Dani's lips curled. "That's a long way from thinking he's capable of murder."

"I told him and Ella that if you'll have me, I'll stick around."

"I will have you."

"Forever?"

She reached for my hand. "Let's see where this goes."

EPILOGUE

Dani

Late December the same year

A dusting of snow fell beyond the windows of the famous Indianapolis steakhouse as the waiter delivered the bottle of the restaurant's finest cabernet sauvignon. The dancing flame from the candle in the middle of our table reflected in Eli's emerald gaze.

"1882 Rutherford," the waiter said, showing us the label.

"The lady is the wine expert," Eli replied. "She can have the first taste."

After pouring a small amount into the glass, the waiter handed it to me.

Holding the slender stem, I swirled the dark-red

liquid. Legs formed inside the glass globe. I inhaled the fruity bouquet with hints of tobacco and mint. The back of my throat pinched as the rich flavor hit my taste buds. "Excellent."

The waiter added more to my glass and added a pour to Eli's glass.

As our waiter walked away, my lips curled. "Drinking alcohol on the job. You are a rule breaker."

"I'm officially off the clock." He lifted his glass. "To spending the rest of our lives breaking the rules."

Our glasses clinked.

Tonight was the date Eli promised me months ago. While we'd had the opportunity to have multiple dates, this one was special. Over the last few months, Eli resigned from Guardian Security and took a job with a local Indianapolis pharmaceutical company, Sinclair. Elijah Rhodes was now the director of security.

After we both took a sip, Eli met my gaze. "I'm serious, Dani. *The rest of our lives.*" He pulled a small velvet box from his magic suit coat pocket.

Tears prickled my eyes, threatening to ruin my makeup as he opened the lid, revealing a large round diamond on a platinum band. "Eli?"

I watched, as if in slow motion, as this giant of a man moved from the chair.

All around us, the diners quieted as whispers of oohs and aahs filled the air. As if covered in a frosted veil, the room disappeared when Eli fell to one knee.

"I hope you don't think this is too soon." His deep

voice resonated. "I refuse to wait to live the life we've planned. I love you, Dani. I'll protect you, love you, and defend you until my last breath. Will you do me the honor of marrying me?"

The dining room held a collective breath as I nodded and attempted to form words. "Yes, I'll marry you." As I reached for Eli's smooth cheeks and pulled his lips to mine, the room erupted in applause.

"I love you, too," I whispered.

Eli slid the ring on the fourth finger of my left hand. "I was going to drop it in your wine glass but thought better of that."

Splaying my fingers, I looked down at the sparkling diamond. "I don't think I'm allergic to diamonds."

His lips quirked as he took the seat across the table and offered me his hand. Our fingers intertwined. "I wasn't willing to take the chance, but I do have the EpiPen if needed."

Throughout the evening, well-meaning patrons came by, offering us their congratulations. As we asked for our check, we were informed that our bill was already paid. When the waiter pointed out the benefactors, Eli and I shook our heads with a scoff.

Damien and Ella waved us toward them.

"There's a speakeasy upstairs," Damien said with a wink as Ella hugged me and whispered congratulations. "Drinks are on me."

The four of us went up the stairs. The room was filled with groupings of soft sofas and cozy chairs.

Chandeliers hung from the ceiling, and a large mahogany bar lined one side of the room. Soft jazz music played from unseen speakers. We went to a grouping marked reserved.

"How did you know where we'd be?" I asked.

My brother winked. "Eli's not the only one who can learn secrets."

When I looked at my fiancé, he grinned. "I may have asked Marsha's permission to marry you. I also didn't swear her to secrecy."

"I hope you don't mind us crashing your evening," Damien said. "Ella and I couldn't pass up the chance to hear your answer. After all, you were there for both of our weddings."

"Both?" Eli asked with a quirk of his eyebrow.

"Both," I replied as I squeezed Damien's hand. "Mom must have said yes. What would you have said?"

Damien looked at Eli and back at me. "Anyone who makes my sister happy, really happy, when the world around her is crumbling, is okay by me."

"How is Mom?" I asked.

"She's a godsend," Ella replied. "Being able to sneak out and be here would be more difficult if she wasn't staying with Dylan. And he loves Hoosier. Duchess, not so much."

I laughed. Duchess was their very spoiled cat.

"Mom wants to go back to Florida after the holidays," Damien said.

"Have you discouraged her?" Eli asked.

Damien shook his head. "Mom's not ready to lose her independence. She knows she has a place to live with us. It's her choice."

I looked at my sister-in-law. "You have done the impossible."

She grinned. "What have I done?"

"You've made this narcissistic asshole actually take other people's feelings into consideration—a feat I never thought was possible."

Ella hugged Damien's arm. "He has his moments."

"Like when he nominated me for the board to take Dad's place."

My brother smiled. "Not nepotism, you're the most qualified. And I was wrong about Mom. She wanted to stay on."

After one round of drinks and a second round of waters, we called it a night.

Although the walk to our condo was only a few blocks, Damien offered to drive. Eli and I chose to walk the quiet city streets as the light snow continued to fall. The circle and streets were decorated with colorful lights, the strings blowing in the wintry wind.

With my hand in Eli's we stood, looking up at the monument.

"I should have waited to propose here."

Warmth filled my cheeks. "I couldn't believe you did it in front of all those people—even Damien and Ella."

"It was a risk." He tugged me until we were facing one another. "You could have said no."

A smile tugged at my lips. "I haven't yet."

Once back to our condo, Eli avoided the lights and turned on the fireplace. Our decorated tree filled with white lights near the windows and the flames were our only illumination.

"Mrs. Rhodes," he said, removing my wool coat.

"Dr. Sinclair."

His lips met mine. "You can be both."

"I can."

Passion radiated from his sexy gaze. "I have a request of my future wife."

My eyebrows quirked. "What kind of request? Am I going to say no?"

"First, I have a question."

Lifting my arms to his shoulders, I asked, "Is it as important as the one you asked earlier?" I wiggled my finger, the diamond sparkling with the fire's glow.

"Secondary to that one. How do you feel about our vows?"

"I don't know what you mean."

"Love, obey, cherish..."

I grinned. "Not a fan of obey. Definitely love and cherish."

"Back to my request." He kissed my nose. "If you were good with obey, I was going to word my request differently."

"Now, you have my curiosity piqued."

"I'd like a fashion show."

Not what I was expecting.

Pressing my lips together, I furrowed my forehead. "What do you want me to wear?"

"Your new ring."

Warmth flooded my circulation. "And?"

"No *and*," he said.

His timbre lowering an octave and reverberating through my circulation caused my nipples to harden. "That's a very specific request."

Eli spun me and lowered the zipper on the back of my dress. "Very specific." His warm breath skirted over my sensitive skin as kisses lavished my neck and shoulders.

My dress slipped from my shoulders followed by the undoing of my bra. My panties were next to go, sliding down to my ankles. Eli dropped again to his knees as he pulled them over my high-heeled shoes.

He looked up with a sexy grin. "I've changed my mind. The shoes stay."

His kisses moved upward from my ankles to my calves and thighs. He inhaled as he reached my core. "You're wet. I smell how sweet you're going to taste."

My breathing shallowed as he continued his exploration, thoroughly tending to each of my breasts, my nipples now as hard as my new diamond.

"You're stunning, Dani."

I gasped when he lifted me and placed my behind on the breakfast bar. I leaned back on my arms, as Eli lifted one of my feet and then the other, placing the shoes on the edge. The fire in his green eyes was inviting and exciting. I'd never felt as vulnerable and as worshipped at the same time.

It was as he released his belt that I tugged on my lower lip. The sound of his zipper echoed through the condo. We'd come together many times since that second night of his assignment. This, however, felt different.

I was fully exposed, and he was fully dressed.

The power shift was erotic.

I called out as we came together.

Pressing myself forward with my arms, I watched as his cock disappeared inside me only to reappear covered in both of our essences. I reached for his shoulders as my feet slipped from the counter.

The friction was too much and not enough. I wanted more as I pushed his suit coat away and tugged at his tie. Once I had his shirt opened, I held tight to his warm shoulders as the volcano within me roared to life. The shooting of sparks, the soaring of flames, the molten lava burst forth as I called out his name and we shattered together.

Eli carried me to the living room and laid me on the soft rug before the fire. When he joined me, he too was naked as he pulled a blanket over us. I laid my head on his shoulder as he wrapped me in his arms.

"Have you proposed before?" I asked. When his gaze met mine, I said, "to Amy?"

He'd shared his past with me, and I'd shared mine. Even though secrets were Eli's specialty, we agreed to not have them between ourselves.

"No. You, Doctor, are my first proposal. Amy and I talked about forever." He hugged me closer. "It's why I didn't want to wait with you. We should seize love when it comes."

I looked again at the beautiful ring. "It would be okay if you had. You don't have to defend love."

Eli rolled me until his nose was millimeters from mine. "Dani, you aren't her. You're not a replacement for her. I wasn't looking for a replacement. I wasn't looking for love." He inhaled. "I wasn't looking for anything except an assignment the afternoon when I walked into Damien's office. I shared my story with you to help you understand why I had my rules."

I nodded. A lump of emotion formed in my throat. It wasn't only what Eli was saying, but that he was sharing such a personal part of himself. The sexy man with the gruff exterior was allowing me to see inside him, the way he'd been looking at my soul since his return.

Eli's tenor lowered. "I will defend my love for you, Dani. Forever and always."

Our lips met.

"Thank you for breaking your rules."

"I love you."

Thank you for reading DEFENDING LOVE.

If you enjoyed this second-chance, steamy, romantic suspense, I recommend the Sinclair Duet: **REMEMBERING PASSION** and **REKINDLING DESIRE** (Damien and Ella's story), The Sin Series, beginning with **RED SIN**, and the Infidelity series—not about cheating—beginning with **BETRAYAL.** Check out all of Aleatha's books and find your new favorite.

What to do now

Visit Aleatha's store to purchase e-books, signed books, and store exclusive items.

LEND IT: Did you enjoy *DEFENDING LOVE*? Do you have a friend who'd enjoy *DEFENDING LOVE*? *DEFENDING LOVE* may be lent one time. Sharing is caring!

RECOMMEND IT: Do you have multiple friends who'd enjoy my dark romance with twists and turns and an all new sexy and infuriating anti-hero? Tell them about it! Call, text, post, tweet...your recommendation is the nicest gift you can give to an author!

REVIEW IT: Tell the world. Please go to the retailer where you purchased this book, as well as Goodreads, and write a review. Please share your thoughts about *DEFENDING LOVE*:

*Amazon, *DEFENDING LOVE*, Customer Reviews

*Barnes & Noble, *DEFENDING LOVE,* Customer Reviews

*Apple Books, *DEFENDING LOVE* Customer Reviews

* BookBub, *DEFENDING LOVE* Customer Reviews

*Goodreads.com/Aleatha Romig

STANDALONE ROMANTIC SUSPENSE:

DEFENDING LOVE

June 2025

BRUTAL VOWS:

NOW AND FOREVER

May 2024

TILL DEATH DO US PART

June 2024

BOUND BY A PROMISE

October 2024

QUEENS AND MONSTERS

January 2025

TO HAVE AND TO HOLD

March 2025

SINCLAIR DUET:

REMEMBERING PASSION

September 2023

REKINDLING DESIRE

October 2023

ROYAL REFLECTIONS SERIES:

RUTHLESS REIGN

November 2022

RESILIENT REIGN

January 2023

RAVISHING REIGN

April 2023

RELEVANT REIGN

June 2023

SIN SERIES:

RED SIN

October 2021

GREEN ENVY

January 2022

GOLD LUST

April 2022

BLACK KNIGHT

June 2022

~

STAND-ALONE ROMANTIC SUSPENSE:

LIGHT DARK

Republished 2024

Previously: INTO THE LIGHT and AWAY FROM THE DARK

SILVER LINING

October 2022

KINGDOM COME

November 2021

~

DEVIL'S SERIES (Duet):

DEVIL'S DEAL

May 2021

ANGEL'S PROMISE

June 2021

SPARROW WEBS

WEB OF SIN:

SECRETS

October 2018

LIES

December 2018

PROMISES

January 2019

TANGLED WEB:

TWISTED

May 2019

OBSESSED

July 2019

BOUND

August 2019

WEB OF DESIRE:

SPARK

Jan. 14, 2020

FLAME

February 25, 2020

ASHES

April 7, 2020

DANGEROUS WEB:

Prequel: "Danger's First Kiss"

DUSK

November 2020

DARK

January 2021

DAWN

February 2021

THE INFIDELITY SERIES:

BETRAYAL

Book #1

October 2015

CUNNING

Book #2

January 2016

DECEPTION

Book #3

May 2016

ENTRAPMENT

Book #4

September 2016

FIDELITY

Book #5

January 2017

THE CONSEQUENCES SERIES:

CONSEQUENCES

(Book #1)

August 2011

TRUTH

(Book #2)

October 2012

CONVICTED

(Book #3)

October 2013

REVEALED

(Book #4)

Previously titled: Behind His Eyes Convicted: The Missing Years

June 2014

BEYOND THE CONSEQUENCES

(Book #5)

January 2015

RIPPLES **(Consequences stand-alone)**

October 2017

CONSEQUENCES COMPANION READS:

BEHIND HIS EYES-CONSEQUENCES

January 2014

BEHIND HIS EYES-TRUTH

March 2014

STAND ALONE MAFIA THRILLER:

PRICE OF HONOR

Available Now

STAND-ALONE YA ROMANTIC THRILLER:

ON THE EDGE

May 2022

~

TALES FROM THE DARK SIDE SERIES:

INSIDIOUS

(All books in this series are stand-alone erotic thrillers)

Released October 2014

~

ALEATHA'S LIGHTER ONES:

PLUS ONE

Stand-alone fun, sexy romance

May 2017

ANOTHER ONE

Stand-alone fun, sexy romance

May 2018

ONE NIGHT

Stand-alone, sexy contemporary romance

September 2017

A SECRET ONE

Prequel to MY ALWAYS ONE

April 2018

MY ALWAYS ONE

Stand-Alone, sexy friends to lovers contemporary romance

July 2021

*QUINTESSENTIALLY THE ONE

Stand-alone, small-town, second-chance, secret baby
contemporary romance

July 2022

*ONE KISS

Stand-alone, small-town, best friend's sister,
grump/sunshine contemporary romance.

July 2023

*ONE STRING

Second-chance, enemies-to-lovers, fake-date, little-sister's-
best-friend, forbidden, stand-alone contemporary romance

July 2024

*All Riverbend interconnected stories

INDULGENCE SERIES:

UNEXPECTED

August 2018

UNCONVENTIONAL

January 2018

UNFORGETTABLE

October 2019

UNDENIABLE

August 2020

ABOUT THE AUTHOR

Visit Aleatha's store to purchase e-books, signed books, and store exclusive items.

Aleatha Romig is a New York Times, Wall Street Journal, and USA Today bestselling author who lives in Indiana, USA. She has raised three children with her high school sweetheart and husband of over thirty years. Before she became a full-time author, she worked days as a dental hygienist and spent her nights writing. Now, when she's not imagining mind-blowing twists and turns, she likes to spend her time with her family and friends. Her other pastimes include reading and creating heroes/anti-heroes who haunt your dreams!

Aleatha impresses with her versatility in writing. She released her first novel, CONSEQUENCES, in August of 2011. CONSEQUENCES, a dark romance, became a bestselling series with five novels and two companions released from 2011 through 2015. The compelling and epic story of Anthony and Claire Rawlings has graced more than half a million e-readers. Her first stand-alone smart, sexy thriller INSIDIOUS was next. Then Aleatha released the five-novel INFIDELITY series, a romantic suspense saga, that took the reading world by storm, the final book landing on three of the top bestseller lists. She ventured into traditional publishing with Thomas and Mercer. Her books INTO THE LIGHT and AWAY FROM THE DARK were published through this mystery/thriller publisher in 2016.

In the spring of 2017, Aleatha again ventured into a different genre with her first fun and sexy stand-alone romantic comedy with the USA Today bestseller PLUS ONE. She continued the "Ones" series with additional standalones, ONE NIGHT, ANOTHER ONE, MY ALWAYS ONE, QUINTESSENTIALLY THE ONE, ONE KISS, and ONE STRING.

If you like fun, sexy, novellas that make your heart pound, try her "Indulgence series" with UNCONVEN-TIONAL. UNEXPECTED, UNFORGETTABLE, and UNDENIABLE.

In 2018 Aleatha returned to her dark romance roots with SPARROW WEBS. And continued with the mafia romance DEVIL'S DUET, and most recently her Brutal Vows series.

You may find all Aleatha's titles on her website.

Aleatha is a "Published Author's Network" member of the Romance Writers of America and PEN America. She is represented by SBR Media and Dani Sanchez with Wildfire Marketing.

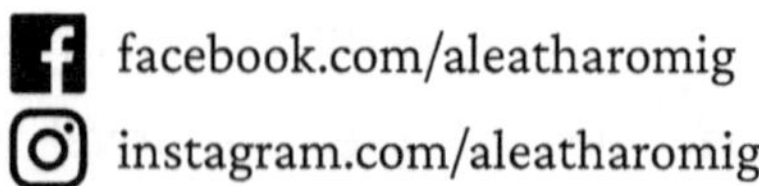